PICKLEBALL IS A PRIORITY!

Acknowledgments

*I wish to thank all those in my personal life
who made this book possible.*

Mr. Nick Productions, LLC
©2023 by Mr. Nick Productions, LLC

Copy Editor – R. Graham

Front cover art – Dr. Mayputz and Kristy Klein
Back cover and spine – Dr. Mayputz and Kristy Klein
Book layout – Kristy Klein / FifteenBlue.com

Photos of pickleball player – Anonymous, or maybe it's me?
Published by Mr. Nick Productions, LLC ©2023

*TRIGGER WARNING –
This book contains words which may trigger laughter*

*This book was NOT written using
Artificial Intelligence or a ghostwriter*

ISBN: 979-8-218-22544-5

Dedication

To my brilliant, athletic, and lawyer son, Alex. You were not only my pickleball hitting partner, but also provided me with rigorous training programs, tactical advice, and emotional support. Thank you.

It wasn't love at first sight, nor was it a repulsive feeling. It was more of an initial sense of confusion and indifference toward a so-called "racquet-sport" which appeared to be as slow as the participants involved. The word "WHY" was top of mind as I sought to fully comprehend the scene of plastic, holed, colored "wiffle balls" being loudly struck by seemingly oversized and hard-surfaced ping pong paddles, wielded mostly by oversized and hard-boiled senior citizens. My bafflement continued as the holey balls hardly flew over the portable nets. Additionally, the elderly doubles players, some of whom barely shuffled around, had grins on their faces. Why were people so happy while playing? Was this a real sport or just some kind of AARP-inspired, physical therapy? And why was the gym so crammed with endless socializing oldsters who patiently waited their turns on the sidelines

for the limited available courts? Then one day I was officially introduced to the game at the local YMCA gymnasium where I had originally witnessed those bizarre goings-on. To wit, ALL my questions were answered when I finally - although at first reluctantly - took up this ridiculously named sport: Pickleball. And then the addiction began! This is not my first bout in the squared circle of the writing realm. Some readers may have already indulged in my previous literary offerings and hopefully found them enjoyable. Although based on the sport of pickleball and the myriad of encountered personalities thereof, this vignette-filled novella is "technically" fictional. It is an observational book of alleged *humor* and should be taken as such. There is no malicious intent; the only intent is to entertain!

Dr. I. Mayputz

I identify as someone who doesn't use the right pronouns.

Table of Contents

Introduction

Who knew that pickleball would become a
bona fide racquet-sport when it was first
"invented" nearly six decades ago on
Bainbridge Island near Seattle? Well, many
savvy people did, but not me. A lifelong
tournament singles tennis competitor and
serious table tennis fanatic from Upstate New
York, and I had never even heard of it. At least
not until fairly recently. Sure, some knowing
folks in my area played all along, however, it
took a while for the sport's insane popularity
to fully crisscross the country and then the
globe. Now that it is so ubiquitous, the rapidly
evolving racquets, balls, attire, footwear,
jargon and rules of the game sometimes make
it challenging to keep up with. In addition,
there are now dedicated indoor and outdoor
venues where it can be played at different skill
levels, by both sexes, in different age
categories, and in singles and doubles.

Presently there are tournaments galore and professionals playing for prize money, not to mention the recent formation of genuine pro teams. Who knew it would get so big? Anyway, let's explore my unexpected conversion from tennis to pickleball and subsequent immersion in the sport. Let's also meet some people who play it. Most names and places have been altered so as not to embarrass the egotistical, infirm, incompetent and downright scurvy. Hopefully you will find the tales within the following pages to be humorous and you will laugh along with me. Maybe at me, as well. And remember: DINK responsibly!

1

What Was All That Racket?

Tennis was still my main game, in addition to wintertime one-on-one basketball, table tennis, and summertime USATF-sanctioned meets involving sprinting and javelin throwing. I had been hitting tennis balls for a long time and basically used the other sports, plus weightlifting, to bolster and condition myself for constantly playing at a high, advanced level. Sure I had a few knee surgeries and aches and pains from all the pounding on-court, but who didn't? All of my so-called tennis buddies were aging, surgically repaired here and there, yet remained feisty and very competitive. We were the best of the best, at least locally, but few ventured out nationally to participate in USTA-sanctioned amateur matches. (Although some did and they did not embarrass themselves.) But most of us were content to pick up national ranking points while continuously bashing each other in our own backyard tournaments. Tennis was still my "thing," in my mind, and something I was good at regardless of my advancing age and infirmities. So, as I was exiting the YMCA weightlifting room one day after doing my usual half hour, no talking, no resting, no nonsense work-out session, I heard a sound I had never heard before: rhythmic and high-pitched thwacking, as if someone was hitting something with a piece of wood. The noise emanated from the basketball gymnasium. But what was it? What was all that racket? Was the gym being refurbished by a group of carpenters, their hammers filling the air with that ungodly cacophony? Could be. I ventured forward out of curiosity to determine the source of that weird discordant dissonance. I opened the door of the gym and stood there transfixed: Below me was a bunch of old timers of both sexes (can you still say that?) *trying* to hit "wiffle balls" at each other over nets placed in the middle of the floor. That was my first impression. But what was it, a form of physical therapy for the elderly, like Zumba? I watched for a few minutes and immediately got the gist of it. The game obviously resembled tennis or ping pong, although played on smaller courts and with solid paddles hitting plastic, holed, balls: hence the ear-splitting sound. Now I knew. In addition, the slow-moving oldsters were lined up in staggered doubles formations opposite each other and seemed to be having a great time. What the hell? They were smiling and jibber-jabbering between points and being cordial to one another? Maybe it was NOT a real sport or competitive? Perhaps that's why everyone looked so happy and relaxed…? I did hear three sets of funny numbers called out loud that didn't make any logical sense, so maybe they did keep score? The shouted numerals were jumbled and sounded all fucked up, yet the players only nodded and continued. Very strange. Anyway, this was not the tennis I was used to, which was often fraught with contested line calls and anger-filled verbal mutterings between points; not to mention the frequent mad outbursts and near physical altercations that sometimes occurred during changeovers. There seemed to be genuine collegiality in this new game I was observing, and I enjoyed seeing the people playing it. I left the Y confused without even knowing the name of what I had just witnessed, still deeply disturbed and puzzled at the scoring system used. And then, another day and another work-out period at the same Y, but this time with my adult son. He is an athletic, smarty-pants, stay-at-home millennial attorney. You know, the usual "basement activist" with a big-ass computer that keeps him ostensibly plugged into the online world of video-gaming and connected to other, self-styled, modern, know-it-alls. I guess I was a bit like him, too, back in the rebellious seventies. However, my brief nose-thumbing attitude at the time consisted of listening to Led Zeppelin, having shoulder-length hair, toking a bit of Columbian Gold and wearing bellbottoms. By contrast, he looks relaxed and retired in his plushy robe and slippers while I have the mental markings of a worn-out, workaholic boomer who barely bumbled and stumbled into retirement. But he is no "loser" in the strict sense of the word. He is straightlaced (he doesn't drink, smoke, dance, nor chew), private prep school and Ivy League educated, law school trained, and has telecommuting jobs with like-minded companies. And though sometimes our ideologies are at opposite ends of the political and philosophical spectrums, I greatly respect and admire him (he is much smarter and more athletically endowed than me). Our mutual love of most major fan-based sports and joint sporting activities somehow bind us together. I take solace in the fact that he is around as my work-out buddy, sparring and athletic training partner. It's not often that an aging boomer gets the luxury of having his adult son so close to home; actually, IN the home! Anyhow, we walked out together from the Y's weight room and both heard the same noise of hard paddles striking plastic spheres. The popping sounds were eerily familiar. However, this time

I raced down to the gym and implored my son to follow. Three people were warming up and perked up when seeing us. They implored one of us to step in as a fourth to play the familiar doubles, as per decorum. I didn't know you could play singles 'til much later. I stepped forward as a would-be sucker and was handed a spare paddle while my son stayed back to observe. He wasn't going to embarrass himself; let the old man do it first. Kind of like Mikey on those old Life Cereal commercials. We foursome proceeded to hit the ball back and forth over the portable net to loosen up and I found I had to unnaturally lunge forward during every shot; the slow-moving plastic ball did not have the same rubbery bounce as a tennis ball and seemed to hang in the air longer. I thought I was struggling mightily in warmup, yet was asked "how long I had been playing pickleball?" Now I knew what this game was called. I was complimented all around by the others who swore that this couldn't be my first time playing. But it was. Some even said that I was a natural. Ha, ha, I had a lot to learn but appreciated the misplaced accolades on my nascent talent. More players appeared and I handed back the paddle and excused myself from the impromptu hitting session. I mentioned pickleball to my son in the car on the way home and he was unimpressed. "Go ahead and hit with those old idiots if you want to. I think you're wasting your time and are way better than they are already," he puckishly stated. "And what about tennis?" he questioned. I didn't reply as we drove home. Pickleball was now on my brain, and I had to find out more about it. I searched and found gobs of info on the internet and quickly picked up the rudiments of the sport online. And it was a SPORT, not a casual and therapeutic pastime for the elderly only. There were athletic males and females (or at least anatomically identified as such) of all ages playing at very high and consistent levels, and I was determined to take that computer screen knowledge and apply it on an actual court. One day as we exited the weight room, I saw an empty gymnasium with the pickleball nets set up, a few paddles and balls lying around and no one playing. I'm not sure what was going on, but I jumped at the opportunity to hit a few green-colored pickleballs. Here was my chance to privately scrutinize the sport with an initially unwilling subject – my son. Although severely visually disabled since birth, his athleticism and winning ways in track and swimming were never questioned. He reluctantly picked up a paddle (he did not play tennis, only table tennis) and we proceeded to bat the ball around a little. He had trouble seeing the pickleball in the dimly lit gymnasium but managed to easily return more than a few of my shots. I was in love; he barely tolerated the brief outing. Soon, actual players started to scuttle into the gym, and we ceased playing and vacated the premises. And that was my first joyous foray into pickleball. I felt exhilarated although my son was still dubious of this "failed" racquet sport. It was January of 2019 and I had doubts about continuing tennis after my last knee surgery in December of 2018. Pickleball appeared out of the blue and seemed to be on the docket as my longstanding tennis-addiction stand-in, but could I take it? I was still wearing a bulky brace on my right knee to prevent hyperextension after the latest chondromalacia clean-out surgery but could adequately move around the small, indoor hardwood courts without much pain. Pickleball seemed the same as tennis although it was "different," but in a good way. And still playing ping pong only bolstered my abilities, reflexes and confidence for this sporty endeavor. Well, I dedicated myself to my newest sport whole hog, eventually shed the knee brace, started playing indoors and outdoors, coerced my wife and recalcitrant son to join me, and never looked back. Of course, my wife fell in love with pickleball, too. My Doubting Thomas son soon realized that he could play at a very high level, outdoors in bright sunlight, and has become a stalwart summertime training and sparring partner for my wife and me. All the noise we now make is music to our ears as we swipe at those different colored pickleballs and enjoy our "new" family sport. And all because I heard that weird, thumping sound at the YMCA years ago and decided to investigate. Curiosity killed the cat, but perhaps playing pickleball will extend my lifespan. Let's hope.

2

The Fall of Tennis

Not to belabor the point, because it has already or will be mentioned many times throughout this book, but my breakup with tennis was quick and easy. But why? After being my "bag" since age nine, I seemed to casually give it up without shedding a soul-searching tear. One day I stuck my customized ProKennex racquets into my pro tennis bag, put the bag on a shelf in the cellar and called it a "career." But why? Probably because I had treated tennis as a "vocation" instead of a sporty hobby. After reaching a high amateur ranking and rating as an older adult, and after my last knee surgery, I realized that I would no longer be able to play at the same level I was accustomed to. That is a very frustrating feeling. But that kind of thinking was because of my love/hate relationship with the game. While "loving" it, I almost breathed a sigh of relief when I stopped playing. Kind of like breaking up with a *hot* but high maintenance girlfriend that I knew I couldn't handle anymore. It's as if my approach to tennis had been as a pro, and I was only too glad to retire. I wasn't a professional, yet my mindset, grueling practice sessions and tournament schedule felt as though I was. None of my local tennis peers and competitors stopped playing, and though slowed down they are still swinging their racquets to this day. But not me; I was finished. My father, who was a professor and successful Division lll college tennis coach, stuck a Wilson Jack Kramer wooden racquet in my hand and I became a "player" at an early age. If he had given me a football or baseball mitt, I undoubtedly would have played a different sport. However, tennis was his "game," and it became mine, for better or worse. Although a former table tennis champion, Dad thought ping pong was a rinky-dink sport and eschewed it in favor of the refined, "country-club-monikered" sport of kings. He was an immigrant, very athletic, and tennis became his instant ticket to respectability among his own European émigrés (most of whom played soccer, what else?) as well as elevating his self-esteem. He had picked it up while in college, became an excellent team "walk-on," and passed on that knowledge to me. Although a great hitter, skillful tactician and frequent tournament player, he cavalierly considered tennis as an exercise as if to downplay his seriousness whenever he lost, which was not often. Nevertheless, I took tennis to heart and early on had delusions of grandeur with the possibility of maybe someday becoming a professional. And not in some dingy club picking up endless fuzzy balls and teaching little old ladies how to serve. I wanted to not only emulate my dad but surpass him in the process. It's a common father-son psychological phenomenon and I was guilty as sin. I wished to someday be like my idol Jimmy Connors. Ha, what a moron I was! While Pop won many local, age-grouped tournaments with ease and little practice, the same cannot be said for me. Plain and simple, I was not as talented as he, plus modern tennis in my age group was changing fast. However, while outwardly considering tennis as just a game, he was always very disappointed in my losing performances. He desperately wanted me to win all the time, yet provided me with little behind-the-scenes resources. I needed more practice, more tactical coaching, more cardiovascular conditioning, more something…. I couldn't just hit a ball around with him a few times a week on the college courts in the summertime only (we played basement ping pong during the long winters) and consider myself well prepared to battle successfully in tournaments. Anyway, his passive-aggressive, ridiculing and mixed messaging-style persisted in my home for years until I went away to university, never fully addressing the psychological damage that had been done or becoming a vaunted tennis star. I never realized my dream of turning professional, not by a long shot. Later in life, after my years in pharmacy college and then dental school, I picked up tennis again, and this time really applied myself. I bought a Tennis Tutor ball machine and shamelessly ingratiated myself onto the local tennis community and joined multiple expensive indoor and outdoor clubs. In my early thirties, I quickly became a feared competitor in my general vicinity and was fully immersed in tennis. It became my "bag" once more. Practicing my strokes, working out, drilling, etc. consumed me athletically and I likened my approach to the one I used in dental school: If you want to pass, all you have to do is the "required amount." However, if you want to get an A+, you have to move heaven and earth. The same went for tennis. Even my aging, but still tennis-playing father remarked favorably at my "new-found" tennis acumen and many tournament victories (age group related, of course). I played a lot and won a lot. I was basically a "pro" without the money, endorsements, accolades or Grand Slam trophies! I then tried unsuccessfully to pass on tennis to my kids. My daughter, although a talented and coordinated athlete, chose not to partake in my browbeating approach, played competitively for a few years, but became a high school track star instead. Tennis was a non-starter for my visually impaired son; his sports were Tae Kwon Do, swimming, and track, in all of which he became very proficient. So, to bond more with my offspring, I also got into track and field events, namely the 100, 200-meter-runs and javelin throwing. This way, I could at least relate to my children's chosen sports, go to their respective track meets with a modicum of appreciation, and root them on. Plus, I had unintentionally started to win at sanctioned USATF track and field events, oftentimes alongside my kids. How cool was that? It was great fun. Nonetheless, tennis was still my main squeeze, besides my wife, and I was always burning the proverbial sports candle down to a nub. Fast forward a few decades and tennis started to bring me great pain, both physically and emotionally, regardless of still winning "elderly" singles and doubles tournaments. By this time my old man was off the hook as a clueless, past mental manipulator and stressor. But the multiple knee surgeries, the right hamstring muscle I tore doing block starts in track, the boredom of repeatedly putting up with the same, clueless local clowns that I had beaten hundreds of times, and the sudden realization that I already had my "day in the sun" all added up to me quitting tennis, just like that. I never looked back. I also saved a pretty penny by quitting all the clubs I had been a dedicated member of for years. Nonetheless, due to hitting endless rubbery and fuzzy green balls, I could very nearly instantly play pickleball and hit plastic, holed green balls with aplomb. So, at the very least I HAVE to thank all those people that were so intimately involved in my previous tennis life.

3

Why Pickleball?

Why pickleball? I say, "Why not?" Pickleball is family friendly, a great form of easy exercise, competitive if need be, fun for all ages and skill levels, and can be played in small spaces, indoors and out. What's not to love? Unless you despise your family, hate to move, hate to compete, and just like to pig out in front of the boob tube while watching three boring hours of baseball - then pickleball is probably not for you. However, if you have even an inkling of trying a social, pseudo-sporty endeavor that won't totally exhaust you (mainly doubles), I would strongly suggest giving it a try, and then getting your family members involved as well. What's the worst that can happen? Besides spending a few bucks on equipment and lessons, you might shed a few pounds, get fit, have fun and then who knows? Competitive tournaments could be just around the corner. The ceiling is high with different available age and skill levels involved and lots of indoor and outdoor places to play. Singles, skinny singles, same-sex and mixed doubles are the formats available. That's the beauty of the sport. Unlike tennis and other racquet sports, pickleball can be played by virtually all and be a satisfying return on investment of time and effort. I can't praise it enough. Plus, the people that you meet are usually like-minded souls and generally friendly types who also gravitated to the sport because of the camaraderie generated around striking a little plastic ball with holes in it. There is no shortage of tutorials on YouTube or certified instructors around that are more than willing to teach the basics as well as advanced techniques. Indoor and outdoor tournaments are proliferating, pro teams are forming and professionals with 5+ ratings are starting to actually make money from the sport. It was fairly easy for me to leave my beloved 50+ year amateur tennis tenure and seamlessly pick up pickleball with virtually little learning curve involved (except for the deftness required for dinking). However, even enthusiasts of ping pong, racquetball, squash, paddle tennis, Padel, platform tennis, handball, as well as non-racquet-wielding, chunky-monkeys can quickly learn, progress, and become formidable opponents. I've personally seen it happen! I say give it a try. And although players are clothed in tennis-familiar outer garments and shoes (although I hear clothing-optional pickleball is now on the upswing), it's generally a cheaper overall sport than tennis, indoor private club fees notwithstanding. There is no need to periodically restring your pickleball paddles - which are usually made of long-lasting, carbon-fiber plastic - and the balls, which do eventually crack or go soft, are inexpensive to buy as compared to replacing constantly worn-out tennis balls. I've said my piece and hopefully have convinced some of you to begin playing, or at least to go to the next level. See you on the courts.

4

Getting Better

Being a competitive fellow in most
things in life, especially sports, I sought
to amp up my pickleball game as
quickly as possible. But you can only
learn so much by watching and
digesting DIY YouTube pickleball
videos where all the mistakes are edited
out, leaving only the smooth and
seemingly effortless winning shots to be
portrayed. How much can one learn
while sitting in front of the computer
screen or playing Virtual Reality Wii
pickleball with a headset on? Not
much, I'm afraid. I had to get up off
my dusty old duff and actually hit a live
ball or two to not only learn, but get

better. Practice makes perfect. Correct instruction from knowledgeable teachers and fellow players willing to give solicited advice is the additional winning formula for success. Carefully watching advanced players and mentally emulating their successful strokes, moves, and tactical decision-making are also valuable self-teaching tools. To reiterate: Playing a lot is important but playing correctly is paramount if improvement is sought. I have seen many "daily" hardcore players who still suck at the game. Believe it or not, I'm also trying to perfect certain aspects of the sport that I feel are lacking in my game while still actively hitting my bread-and-butter shots in the process. My old man, who was a tenured professor and tennis coach at our hometown college, spent years correcting and improving my forehand and backhand strokes until I took over that effort and then tweaked them slightly for the changing topspin game. I was young, belligerent and cocksure, leading to many arguments with him, but I grudgingly accepted his years of coaching wisdom and at least learned the fundamental basics of proper form and function. The same applies to pickleball. Again, the obvious advice is to learn how to play correctly in the first place. Take lessons, study other players in action, and scour the internet for DIY tutorials. Immediately try to learn the backhand slice as well as the backhand topspin drive from the backcourt. In other words: learn how to hit the backhand! Enough preaching,

you know what I'm saying. When I
decided to wholly convert to pickleball
as my go-to racquet sport (in addition
to table tennis), I immersed myself in
it. Being somewhat of a determined
cuss (what else is new?), I quickly found
out about playing venues and the levels
of play offered there. Because I already
had a modicum of supposed talent, I
basically foisted myself onto the
established groups in various locations
in my area. Well, I'm sure some
advanced players took umbrage at my
boldness and alleged hubris, but most
let me in and luckily, I did not
disappoint them with initially subpar
play. Even though I started out as the
worst of foursomes before my capital
rapidly shot up, I noticed all the eye-
rolling fellows who put up with my

early lack of pickleball prowess. Thank you! After starting to play at the local YMCA that first got me hooked on the sport, seasoned elders who recognized my potential suggested I branch out as soon as possible to keep improving. Thusly - and even though wearing a prescription anti-hyperextension knee brace on my right knee after my latest repair surgery - I ended up playing in an all-girls private academy (the five dollar walk-on fee, weekend pickleball program for outsiders was supervised by the female assistant dean who was also a national singles pickleball champ), in area community centers, in other YMCA's and in an old, filthy, dimly lit church basement where the area's top pickleballers would "discretely and secretly" play (you had to be in the know to be invited by this select and snooty bunch). Well, that last venue was not THAT exclusive, but the area's top players sure made it feel like it was. Many churches had mini gymnasiums and this popular Baptist church was no exception. Three bucks allowed you to play doubles for an hour and a half. Other people played there as well, however, a newbie had to be highly recommended to join the "elite cabal" and be officially invited to play on certain days and times. Kind of like joining a secret society or something. It was legit and merit-based, but many novices protested: How could one improve if good players froze out beginners and only played with each other? Anyway, I had received a cryptic email one day explaining the hierarchy

of the Church-play and was asked to
join this hallowed group. I immediately
accepted. The trusted and fearless
leader, who had the key to the church
basement, set the day and time and
only the first five responding players
would get a spot to play. There were
around twenty or so in this cadre (male
and female) and it was doubles only.
Four would play while the fifth would
rotate in after each game. That way
everyone got a chance to rest. This is
where I really learned how to play the
game at the highest level. Even though
the hardwood floor was dirty, with a
torn portable net and lights barely
shining from the high ceiling, the level
of play was outstanding. And though
my newfound besties appreciated my
athleticism and big-time strokes, I did

not yet possess the finesse and racket-head speed at net that are the usual hallmarks of accomplished doubles players. I methodically picked up good habits, the needed vernacular (dinks, slams, kitchen, etc.) and started winning more and more, regardless of who my partner was. Soon, I was considered a "good" player by the others, and a reliable doubles partner regardless of my obvious tennis-influenced skills and instincts. Nevertheless, I still had a lot to learn. The finer nuances of the sport in doubles escaped me for now, however I kept at it. Additionally, now that I had finally shed the limiting knee brace and could run again, singles action was my next goal (I had been primarily a singles tennis player). And in singles, it turned out that I could use a combination of my tennis and table tennis abilities to bash balls with great effect. For me, doubles is fun, but only when hitting with good partners and if played at a high level. All in all, my pickleball learning curve was fast and easy, as it is for most folks. Being an athlete is not a requirement, nor is great coordination or on-court movement. Many jaded and jealous tennis pros call pickleball an abomination and unabashed, adulterated tennis. And I would have to agree. True tennis proficiency takes years of effort and has many neuro-muscular moving parts to memorize, such as overhand serving. However, a few short lessons later and a person can be playing *respectable* pickleball, instantly enjoying themselves. How great is that?

5

Inspirations

I've had many teachers, including non-interactive DIY YouTube videos, who have had patience with my developing game while putting up with my quirky personality and provocative mouth. Thank you. And a special shout out to the individuals who unknowingly and knowingly honed my pickleball skills and who I feel compelled to mention, albeit using initials only. As previously stated, my journey began in January of 2019. So, my first encounter was with the indoor pickleball crowd, most of whom play outdoors as well. Anyway, one wintry day I was in my dental office, a few months prior to my retirement, when I happened to do a customary six-month oral hygiene examination on an old buddy and former tennis competitor. As always, we spoke briefly about our old tennis days and ribbed each other about who had more victories over one another. Near the end of the exam, E. suddenly blurted out that while his daughter was fully immersed in tennis as a budding and talented junior star, he had abandoned the game as a player in lieu of pickleball. Although younger than me, he had made the conversion and only coached tennis at this point. As he was leaving, E. told me to get ahold of him so we could play pickleball. I was elated, but told him that I was a novice at best. Although a formerly fearsome tennis player, I would be no match for him. He was not deterred and even suggested what paddle and shoes I should purchase. Of course, I took him up on his offer to play with me and thanked him for all the equipment advice. And I thank him to this day for smoothing the way and introducing me to his cronies, the various indoor facilities available at the time, and encouraging me to become an advanced player. Thanks E. Next came S., a coach and dean of student affairs at an all-girls private high school. Before the Covid pandemic, she loosely organized Saturday pickleball play at the school's spacious gymnasium for outsiders who would pony up five bucks apiece to play doubles for a few hours. She had eight portable nets set up and the place was still packed with people, with a waiting line in effect. Of course, lefty S. was a tremendous pickleball player in her own right. She was a formidable and former women's 50-55-year-old singles national champ and boy was she good! I learned a lot not only through playing, but also through scrutinizing her exceptional athleticism and approach to the game. She was equally gifted in singles and doubles and always had complimentary remarks for the mixed crowd at hand. Men and women of all ages played there, and I am thankful for her frank remarks about my up-and-coming game. The pandemic ended up closing down the school and our pickleball play. S. and I have unfortunately lost touch. W. is an older gentleman I met at the YMCA closest to my house. He was in his late seventies and to date had more than a few joint replacements in his body. Small, wiry and very athletic, his multiple prosthetic joints hardly slowed him down. He was a former two-time NCAA national wrestling champion and that kind of grit and determination from his halcyon college grappling days showed on the pickleball court. He was one tough cookie to beat, regardless of his age and seeming infirmity. Always quite the talker, he must have seen some kind of talent in my game and tried to arrange the waiting paddles so that we could hit against each other when it was our turn to play doubles. He tutored me with his constant commentary, praise, and coaching abilities. Thank you, W. His good buddy and sometime tournament doubles partner was the insufferable J. He is an elderly, hefty, lefty human specimen, yet his garrulous but kindly demeanor was much appreciated by all. J. would always slowly lumber up to the kitchen line on most points and was a burly presence on the courts. Early on he made sure to give me honest and useful opinions in a forceful way while smiling from ear to ear. How could you get mad at someone that was quick to grin and laugh? And one who would pick up the ball with a PickleUpper cup mounted on the butt of his paddle. However, he could not get around as well as he would have liked due to a balky left hip, which he recently had replaced. Hopefully his mobility has been somewhat restored, but there is no escaping the aging process. Thank you,

J. for making pickleball all about fun, in spite of always trying to win. B. was in his early eighties when we first interacted on the indoor YMCA courts. A lanky and seasoned player, I was immediately struck by his quick hands at net and his ability to topspin-flick the ball while positioned at the kitchen line. That was something I had seen pros do and was an ability I have only recently mastered. Self-effacing and humble, I later heard that he had won many tournaments with various doubles partners and was a fixture in the area's pickleball community. He is competitive, relentless and has that innate positive energy. While watching him you can tell that he wishes he had the legs of a younger man to compliment his honed strokes and magnificent overall game. It is always a pleasure to play with or against him. And not to forget about the other J. With his patented high socks, he was always prepared for all-day pickleball at any and all venues. His gregarious nature and boundless enthusiasm can be overwhelming, however. Possessing a hard, sidespin serve and switching hands depending on which side of his body the pickleball is at, J. sets a new standard for making pickleball look effortless. Thanks J., for always making me feel welcome and giving me tips that I can't use. Lol. Don't worry J., we love you. I first met older gentleman V. at the local YMCA and marveled at his all-court game in doubles. He liked to win and literally flew around his doubles partners so he could hit the winning shots. As I progressed up the ladder of ability, I enjoyed playing with and against him. It was always a hoot to hear his mutterings whenever he missed, which was not often. And, lastly, there was the advanced-level cohort of tournament players that welcomed me and my "mouth" at the City Baptist Church (yes, many large churches of all denominations usually have a small gym). I was grateful for their court knowledge and continued tutelage of yours truly, at least in doubles. Those were some serious sessions of pickleball, with more hitting than talking, even from me. But thanks to Covid and the lockdowns, I lost touch with most of those special players such as L, P, the other P, R, A, K, M, F, E and others, and have only recently reconnected with some of them at different places. Most of the above mentioned pickleballers are year-round tournament-ready gladiators and always "on tour." Anyhow, as I have progressed in my pickleball journey, hopefully I too have become somewhat of an inspiration and not a constant bane or consternation to other players! But there are two more people that I HAVE to mention, and they are my wife and son. During the Covid pandemic, family time became paramount and cherished. It seems my departure from tennis was fortuitous because I was no longer consumed with selfish singles struggles playing against the same male goofballs. Now I could consistently play a "kinder and gentler" racquet sport with my wife and son, and that paradigm shift alone made us stronger as a family unit (my adult daughter also plays but she and her family live three hours away). My wife was an inconsistent and itinerant tennis player and never felt comfortable playing the game and enjoyed it less and less as she aged. And then the magic of pickleball swallowed her up. Immediately after I gifted her a brand new ProKennex Kinetic paddle (she now plays with Gearbox paddles like me), she took to the sport like a vulture to carrion and continues to be my singles sparring partner as well as to play with many newly made friends. Additionally, all her previous tennis skills paid off handsomely. She is a solid intermediate player and is still improving. My adult lawyer son was a standout high school athlete (swimming and sprinting) and has a high-level, Olympic style, table tennis game. So, after that fateful time at the local Y, when we casually batted around a pickleball in the gym for a few minutes, I asked him if he wanted to pick up the sport for real. He eventually agreed and has become my stalwart training partner, physio, tournament traveling companion, and biggest fan. Almost daily outdoor training sessions during the summer have made both of us much better players. Although his limited vision prevents him from effectively playing indoors or at the net (he can't quite pick up the pickleball fast enough), he can nonetheless see the ball well enough in bright sunlight from the backcourt to occasionally beat me in head-to-head matches. Anyway, he currently uses a custom-weighted (by yours truly) Prince Response Pro pickleball paddle and loves it. I haven't made him a Gearbox convert, yet…. I am truly grateful for all the people who inspired me to keep striking that holey plastic ball and have put up with my sometime acerbic, eccentric and eclectic on-court mannerisms. Thank you one and all.

6

The Nitty Gritty

That title is not to be confused with the 1963 hit song recorded by Shirley Ellis, or the Nitty Gritty Dirt Band of *Mr. Bojangles'* fame. No, the intent is to briefly comment on some of the *granular* (thank you, debunked Dr. Birx) aspects of pickleball. I'd like to briefly and lightly explore the assortment of paddles and balls available, attire worn, strokes used, and thought processes involved when hitting that hard, plastic, holed orb. Now, I'm not a pro; nor have I played for a lifetime like some folks. That being said, my extensive tournament tennis background, racquet sport enthusiasm and observations have made me "somewhat" qualified to at least give MY limited two cents about pickleball. Plus, I do have a wee bit of *street cred* having won more than a few state singles pickleball titles at a high level.… Here goes nothing: After my seemingly overnight conversion from tennis to pickleball, and the resultant "baptism by fire," I took to this "new" racquet sport like a burrowing woodchuck does to his new hole in the ground: with a mixture of trepidation and optimism. First and foremost was to decide on what kind of paddle to purchase. And boy, there were a lot of choices. Thick, thin, edgeless, edged, long-handled, short-handled, smooth, textured, heavy, medium, light, teardrop shaped, regular boxy-shaped, honeycombed interior, solid graphite, ribbed or with a receptacle end. Wait a second, those last two were prophylactic references and I'm sorry if I offended anyone. Not! Anyway, the possible alternatives were endless. Like in other sports, sales gimmicks supported by supposed "pros" hawk one brand and type over another in slick tutorials and testimonials. I remember having gone through – and paid for – multitudes of tennis racquets, each time being influenced by the promises of my game being greatly improved. If only I had those certain "magic sticks" that McEnroe, Connors or Borg used – I would be all set. What hogwash. Sadly, it was all hype. Even with a new piece of technology in my hands, I was still a wannabe and not an instant champion!

And no one initially told me that custom and secretive modifications were carried out on the professional tennis racquets as to the specific requirements of the player. The racquets sold off the store shelf even in those bygone days were not the exact ones played with by the pros. But I eventually got savvy and learned what to do with the store-bought models. I ended up strategically lead-weighting my tennis racquets over the years. However, there was also so much placebo psychology involved that I don't know if my customization of newly bought racquets really improved my abilities or not. I think I got better, at least to a point. But it was hard to tell for sure. Anyhow, I didn't want to fall into the same trap with pickleball, always searching and buying the latest and greatest because of FOMO. Pickleball Central, the online superstore out of Washington State for all things pickleball, has nearly every paddle on the market and scrolling through the myriad images and endorsements can be mind boggling and mood altering. Where do you start? Should you phone a friend, try a demo paddle, check out what the pros are using or what the best player at your local Y is hitting with? Wow… decisions, decisions. Suffice it to say that there are two basic types of paddles – honeycombed ("composite") and solid ("graphite"). The reason I have them in quotes is because there are so many hybrid variations now available. And both can have modifications to further be distinguished as power or control paddles with various spin rates. However, those statements are an oversimplification and generalization. Some are even marketed as "quiet" paddles, intended to be used near housing developments. The length and weight of the paddle are also important factors to consider. But where do you begin, and should a paddle be legally tinkered with after purchasing it? I always preferred a "heavy" tennis racquet rather than the stock models available for mortals. Hence, after purchase, I would remove the butt cap and glue one or two one-ounce, fishing sinkers into the handle. This made a standard, store-bought tennis racquet at least two ounces heavier and perfect for my power game. I also strategically added lead tape around the frame to make sure the "stick" was balanced. In a tennis stroke, you lead with the wrist and the extra heft in the handle carries the momentum forward without compromising the swing weight too much. That kind of physics and logic apply to pickleball paddles as well. Lead tape applied to the periphery of the paddle and under the handle's grip is how I modestly modify my pickleball bat. It now weighs approximately two ounces more than a store-bought 8.5-ounce one, is evenly balanced, and gives me extra pop in singles. The obvious downside is the extra weight! It can be slightly unwieldly in fast-paced doubles action at the net but years of playing with weighted objects in my hand have conditioned my reflexes to compensate for the increased heaviness. But it takes time to get used to and is not for everyone. My forehand and backhand are a cross between tennis and ping pong strokes and seem to suit me. Some players slap at the ball, but I use traditional tennis swings that I learned years ago, only slightly modified for pickleball. And remember, NOTHING can be applied to the faces of the paddle to enhance the texture and playability: no decals, no rubber, no Stickum, and no Biden *"I Did That"* stickers. For me, the brand and type of paddle was secondary to the weight. Upon the recommendation of my initial mentors, I purchased an expensive, edged composite model, then doctored it up and started playing. Experimentation was the key, at least at first. I instinctively knew what I wanted and three paddles later I settled upon a standard-sized thin "graphite," edgeless one that I willfully *augmented*. It gives me lots of "extra" power and spin. I can still dink and hit drop shots effectively, even with this heavyweight in hand. Though not cheap at a few hundred dollars, it does not have to be periodically restrung and both surfaces are holding up well in spite of the near daily hard pounding they take. I believe pricy pickleball bats are worth the investment and can provide years of carefree service, unless smashed, chipped or delaminated by a well-meaning doubles partner while both of you are going for that dang middle ball at the same time. Pickleballs for indoor/ outdoor use and tournament play were once dominated by a few companies. However, like the paddles which many tennis companies have wisely started to manufacture, the balls also are now made by "major" racquet-sport manufacturers and sold in the pickleball marketplace. Onix and Juggs were once considered the gold standards, but currently the Franklin X-40 is the official ball used in many outdoor tournaments, including by the Professional Pickleball Association. However, that may change as well. Gamma, Penn, etc. are all in the market and may become one of the next "best" balls to use. I will say that after having played even for a short while, I can quickly discern if a pickleball is too light, not perfectly circular, too soft, cracked, or a cheap knockoff from the name brands. Thusly, many hardcore pickleballers come prepared with their own balls (even women) and are more than ready to whip them out as needed to play "correctly." But wait just a minute. Let's describe the way the balls behave, or don't. Pickleballs are not tennis balls. Instead, they are light, hard and holey plastic shells that barely bounce. As a newcomer to the sport, the constant last-minute lunging to hit the ball caused me disconcerting lower back and leg tightness and discomfort. The usual hunched and falling-forward stance when striking a ball that is below knee level is proper form but can be a frustrating concept to grasp at the beginning. And the lower back continues to get a workout due to picking up the balls off the ground between points. In tennis, a technique used to trap and lift the ball against a foot by the long racquet cannot be utilized in pickleball. Repeatedly bending over to grasp the pickleball often results in a voluntary backache. Of course, after playing awhile the body readily adjusts to the various "new" positions that are required to play effectively. But before active play begins there is a customary warm-up period where players stand at the kitchen line and gently exchange back and forth hits that land in the NVZ (no volley zone, or Kitchen). Then most hit the ball at each other from the air to practice the volley before stepping back and hitting a few shots from the baseline. It's how the pros warm up as well. A word about attire and shoes:

Nothing special - shorts, shirts, head and wrist sweatbands, caps, and a decent, light pair of tennis kicks with reinforced soles with good grip, whether for indoor or outdoor use. Sometimes, however, indoor shoes with "sticky" gum rubber bottoms are preferred. The last topic I will briefly touch upon is the mental aspects of playing pickleball. Not that I am a psychologist, sociologist or even a mentalist - maybe just mental - but here goes: Although the addictive aspect of this "easy" racquet sport will be touched on later, there is something very positive and uplifting about striking a light, plastic, holed ball to and fro over a net while surrounded by friendly humans. The mesmerizing fast pace of advanced play greatly appeals to me, and I often find myself "in the zone" (terminology used to describe an athlete who plays almost unconsciously and brilliantly due to hyper concentration and with the added ability to dissociate oneself from outside interference) more frequently than I did while playing tennis. Oftentimes I will forget the score between points or for how long I have been playing. And then I will snap out of the "pickleball trance" only to go back into it again. It is a great feeling, like a runner's high, and somewhat difficult to explain. It doesn't matter because playing pickleball scrambles my brain chemicals in a delightful way and I love it.

7

Serving and Returning

In tennis, serving players receive two chances. Not so in pickleball as each serve counts. But after all, it's an underhand serve. How hard can it be to goof up? Well, let's not debate the difficulty, but touch on the importance of it. And, since some of the earlier rules have been relaxed lately, serving is suddenly a hot topic in pickleball circles. It can be accomplished by hitting the released ball or by dropping the ball to bounce first – the "Drop Serve." No, the ball cannot be forcibly bounced, only passively dropped from any height as deemed necessary. The Chainsaw serve is now illegal, meaning that a player cannot spin the ball prior to striking it during the serve. Sure, one can put "English" on the ball, but only with the paddle. With all this being said, is serving really that important in pickleball? Well, purists and some pros will counter that serving is merely a way to start the point and not a way to score a point. I beg to differ, especially when it comes to singles play. Much like in tennis, placing the ball around the box and varying the speeds and spins can be very effective in scoring cheap points. Or, at the very least to handcuff a worthy opponent and mitigate the return. Topspin, sidespin, and underspin serves are now legal and used by many players, including professionals. I recommend a reliable and hard topspin serve - my go-to weapon of choice. It is hard to tee off from and I can usually anticipate the type of return I will get. Now a few words about the return game. Since the server has to let the ball bounce before hitting it back, the returner in pickleball has the initial advantage at winning the point to get a Side-Out. Various strategies and strokes such as chip-and-charge, deep returns, slices or hard topspins can be utilized on the incoming serve. But do something. The return is an opportunity to place the serving player (or team) in jeopardy. And it does not have to be an outright winner. However, making the server immediately move when playing singles can be most efficacious, no matter the pace of the returned shot. And in doubles, the prized down-the-middle return shot is often one of the standard formulas for success.

8

Volleys

Having been on the receiving end of many slam-banged pickleballs makes it seem as though EVERYONE knows how and when to volley. But au contraire. Sometimes a dink should be used, especially if an opponent is playing back. Sometimes a put-away shot should be employed. It's all a judgement call during the heated battle, both in doubles and singles. In tennis, a slightly downward punch is the preferred stroke when hitting a winning volley. It prevents the ball from sailing and gives the hitter control. In pickleball, the same kill-shot is preferably produced with a flat hit or with a topspin backhand or forehand flick, for maximum effect. Because the ball is light, the extra spin generated helps prevent a return. Nevertheless, the quickness required to snap the wrist over the ball at the kitchen line takes much practice. Most professionals have the shot. I learned it in ping pong as a child and carried it over into pickleball, but it is hard to do during a game. It takes timing and effort to execute correctly. Of course, if there is a sitter waiting to be blasted, by all means just hit the damn ball, and hit it hard. But as everyone knows, volleying from the air while standing inside the kitchen area is illegal in pickleball. And now a few brief words about overheads: they are basically overgrown volleys to be hit with an overhand-like tennis service motion. Unless one is a quick study, lessons are advised for most non-racquet playing individuals who wish to properly master the mechanics and footwork of an overhead smash. Because nothing is uglier or more embarrassing than missing a poorly timed overhead. Balancing the body while backpedaling and simultaneously striking the ball can be tricky business and downright dangerous. Pros make the "easy" overhead winner look effortless. Trust me, it is not.

TIMEOUT!

9

Outdoor vs. Indoor

Like night and day, or the difference between Oscar Madison and Felix Unger (the mismatched roommates from yesteryear's TV sit-com "The Odd Couple"), outdoor and indoor pickleball can be contrasting sports. Although the overall play and scoring are the same, there are stark disparities between the two. A major variation is the ball used. Unlike in tennis or most other "ball sports," pickleball employs two types of plastic orbs. The indoor ball has twenty-four holes and is slightly softer than the forty-holed outdoor version. Pickleballs are lightweight plastic and very prone to deleterious outdoor elements such as wind. Therefore, more but smaller holes as well as heaviness and stiffness contribute to the stability and flight of the outside sphere. After all, it is still a wiffle ball at heart. The indoor ball is unaffected by breezes, only the color is paramount so it can be adequately visualized by the old fogies. Orange, red or yellow are the preferred hues used in gymnasiums whereas optic green or neon yellow balls are frequented out-of-doors. There are other colors of course, but those are the most popular iterations of the pickleballs put-to-use. Secondly, the biggest difference between the two opposing venues is the slipperiness of the courts. Whereas outdoor ones tend to be gritty (a la tennis courts), the inside, highly glossed, wooden or linoleum gym floors are smooth. This makes for a challenging time if alternating play between surfaces. The worn bodily attire is basically and seasonally the same, except for the footwear. Whereas indoor kicks are purposely designed with "stickier" bottoms (sometimes gum rubber) to provide purchase on often slippery surfaces, outdoor sneaks are a hardier version of tennis shoes, with reinforced and durable outer soles for added grippage when playing on rough courts. Plus, the quick, start-stop movements required in advanced pickleball, in both singles and doubles, make for very important footgear decisions by the player. All in all, I would say that going between outdoor and indoor pickleball necessitates the wearing of disparate shoes not only to compensate for the vastly dissimilar courts but to adequately protect the feet. When playing outdoors in hot, sunny weather, I usually wear baseball-style hats and sunglasses. Indoors, the same caps are worn backwards, and protective eyewear completes my ensemble. However, outdoors play can be a real bitch. The sweltering heat, the wind gusts trying to tip over the portable nets (any wind over 10 mph starts to be annoying), humidity, fog, rain, searing sun, background distractions, and non-uniform or cracked asphalt playing surfaces can be distracting or downright bullshit. In other words, the controlled and quiet indoor environment (except for the popping of the balls) can be a more forgiving and rewarding experience than putting up with outdoor nonsense. However, I grew up playing outdoor tennis only and got used to the accompanying crap. I remember sarcastically remarking to my old man many times that if we got one summer day of playing without wind or humidity it was a small victory, and we should savor it. Such were the weather patterns of the Catskills at the time. The same goes with playing pickleball in the raw outdoors. Now, I have been mentioning the word "courts" throughout this vignette. But to date I have not played on a real, honest-to-goodness, indoor or outdoor pickleball court! Either existing tennis courts have had pickleball lines taped or painted on them or existing gymnasium floors have lines on them delineating the pickleball court boundaries. The indoor facility floors can sometimes have so many lines on them, and in many colors, that it can become confusing and frustrating for old farts to play. Pros usually engage on officially designated and specifically built pickleball courts and more of these are being constructed around the country. But for now, pickleball is making tennis courts and indoor basketball/volleyball courts great again. And one more thing: When playing doubles in tennis, the doubles alleys and outermost lines are used. In pickleball, the same set of lines are used for singles and doubles.

10

Bangers....

In my relatively short experience with pickleball I have observed that beginners tend to bang the ball as the stroke of choice. Obviously when starting out, and without a racquet sport background, the tendency is to just make contact and get the dang ball over the net. And without formal lessons, the next tendency is to end the point as quickly as possible. Banging the ball with little regard for proper placement works well for a while until you run into players with great hand skills that will return most every shot and then some. So, should the banging escalate and end up sounding like male woodpeckers trying to attract a mate by endless drumming against dry wood? Or should novice players purposely seek to slow the game down into a semblance of thoughtful point construction and artful ball striking to win points? Singles pickleball, like singles tennis, has always been about hitting the ball to "where they ain't," including serving and volleying. But advanced-level doubles pickleball traditionally has been about judicious dinking, careful ball placement and outfoxing the opposition. However, I now see more hard-striking and driving of the ball in elite doubles circles as well, especially for the third shot, or when an adversary is caught in no-man's land or at the baseline. The third shot dink is still executed, but not as frequently. The hard-hitting, NVZ-net exchanges by fast-handed players are a delight to watch and partake in, but I believe the overall game is slipping toward tennis regardless of the finesse and ball control exhibited by pros, many of whom were former tennis players. As a former big-striking, baseline tennis banger, I brought the same physicality and high-octane game to singles pickleball and have done well in tournaments. However, doubles is another animal and mindset. But I'm not sure if doubles pickleball will continue to embrace the strategically methodical yet frequently plodding dinking game. The pros sure seem to love it, but at the beginner and novice levels not only do you require patience and a different approach, but the reward gained may be minimal. It's easier to endlessly bang away like a woodpecker to win the points. Nevertheless, as in most sports, evolution rules. Tennis changed rapidly and radically during my fifty years in the game, and I am confident that pickleball will as well. Perhaps in the future, advanced players will fit right in with the paltry poppers, at least in the bashing style of hitting that damn ball.

11

Sitting Duck

We've all inadvertently done it - even me, darn it. But not on purpose, mind you. However, shit happens and shitty shots can occur at any time, especially during doubles play. You are standing there at the ready just past the kitchen line, with your head and paddle pointed forward, anticipating a dink at any moment then – WHAM, you get tagged in the groin out of nowhere. Ouch! Well, not out of nowhere, but because of an elevated "pop-up" shot from your partner that was too high over the net and just sat up there like an Andy Petitte hanging curveball of yesteryear, ready to be struck with gusto by a grateful opposing player. We've all been both the perpetrator and receiver of said pickleball assault. Many times, the clearly better player of the twosome is the one that purposely gets drilled by the slam, as if to knock her ego down a peg or two. Sometimes it's just too late to react fast enough and the ball will be eaten! And often it is done with glee and great relish by the "friendly" foe across the net who would love to see a good player get her supposed comeuppance. I hate being a targeted patsy, but unfortunately it is a very common occurrence, especially at the novice level. After being lulled into boredom at the NVZ line, I often get the last winning shot struck at me full force as if to reinforce my vulnerability and to discount any advanced skill that

I may possess. It's always an ego boost to handcuff a good player and watch her ungracefully lose a point. I love a good high ball to drink or hit, but NOT being on the receiving end over and over when it is viciously banged at me. Actually, even "religious Dinkers" wait for the pop-up and then spike the ball across the net at the feet of the opposition. It is a legitimate winning pickleball strategy when played right, however, the advanced players seem to sense when the kill shot is coming and rarely are blindsided by a ball slammed into their left ear holes. It is at the intermediate and lower levels that players frequently set up their hapless partners for annoying and sometimes painful bodily "tattoos." The obvious answer would be to stay back and away from the kitchen. Well, then you could be burned by a drop-shot dink or limit yourself for your own put-away. The only viable solution is to improve your game and hand speed (most advanced players can return balls sharply hit at them at point blank range) and play at a level where you and your partner trust each other. That will lead to less popped-up gopher balls, because no one likes a floater except to flush one!

12

"See Something, DON'T Say Something!"

The title is a sarcastic rebuttal to former communist East Germany whose citizens were urged to tattle on family members, friends and neighbors. Our own "benevolent" government wants us to "see something and then say something." Ha. Whistleblowers usually get punished and not rewarded, remember? Instead, the above title should be prominently displayed at all pickleball venues. Simply put, unless you are giving paid-for lessons, be careful acting as a coach or teacher to someone who might not appreciate being lectured while playing. Unless that person specifically asks you to offer

strategic or shot-making advice, zip it,
- as Morton Downey Jr. often said.
Nothing ruins an outing, friendship or
marriage faster than well-intentioned
but unsolicited advice from a doubles
partner or opponent. Especially if it
keeps on coming throughout the game,
or even afterwards. The closeness of
doubles pickleball and the mostly
elderly combatants have helped foster
an overall culture of friendliness and
camaraderie. But like the old saying
goes: Familiarity brings contempt. I
remember butting heads with my old
man while he was impatiently trying to
teach me tennis in the early 1970s.
Frustration bubbled over from both of
us, and he was a legitimate college
tennis coach with teams that won
regional championships year after year.

And here his own athletic but temperamental (more mental than temper) son was giving him lip. Good grief. I admit that I was also impatient and absolutely hated to be correctly criticized. In hindsight, it was mostly my fault. I wanted to play with a semi-western grip to put more topspin and torque on the ball. Dad was stuck playing like Stan Smith and teaching his elegant yet less penetrating strokes. I wished to learn a big serve like Roscoe Tanners'; Dad instead taught a functional serve that was less flashy but reliable. Many ensuing verbal fights on and off the tennis courts could have been avoided if both of us had been more understanding of one another and the changing racquets and times. But I will say that Pop did produce an excellent tennis-playing son, although it took SENIOR singles championships to finally extract the full benefits of all that torturous juvenile training. Anyway, very few people like to be told what to do. In doubles pickleball, the urge to "correct" a flaw in a lesser partner's game can be understandably and undeniably strong, but don't do it. If your wife pleadingly and sincerely asks why she keeps missing the dreaded half volleys or dinks, then MAYBE and GENTLY suggest a remedy. Otherwise, bullheaded criticism can be a recipe for hard feelings often leading to things not getting hard, if you know what I mean. Enough said. But let's examine at least some of the most egregious acts on-court that should be avoided so as NOT to be pestered by a well-meaning

: Don't ever forget the Double Bounce rule and try to serve and volley like in tennis. The returned serve must bounce on your side before the ball can be struck. And speaking of serving, it is underhanded and not that difficult to learn. With the new "Drop Serve" option there is no excuse for not getting the ball in play. Serving faults should be rare, but sometimes hitting advanced, extra hard serves close to the lines can induce errors. Anyway, typical serving SHOULD be easy and not a chore. Smashing balls, whether as a true overhead shot or slamming at the kitchen line SHOULD be a satisfying and point ending endeavor. But not always. Remember, the ball is lightweight and slow moving. And the opposition may be very good or very

lucky at returning the walloped balls.
Worse yet, sometimes an "easy" ball
that should be put away is muffed by
over-eagerness. In other words, blast
that easy sitter judiciously to win the
point. In doubles, taking the midline
shots as the forehand player in the add
court is the customary practice.
However, that is something that should
be discussed with the partner
beforehand. There are instances where a
partner's backhand is strong and could
conceivably be the go-to stroke to
return those pesky down-the-middle
shots. Of course, hitting down the
middle is the bread and butter of sound
pickleball play and where many points
are won, regardless of who takes
"command" of the shots. Another point
to address is taking, or at least swinging

at, balls that are clearly going out. Sometimes it cannot be helped, especially if the ball is hit at your head or looks close to landing in. It takes time to develop prudent judgment to determine the projected flight of the ball. Many times, a seasoned doubles partner will loudly call out, "Let it go," as a rude but necessary reminder during a hotly contested point. The obvious danger of swatting at "out" balls is making mistakes or hitting the ball back and giving opponents a second chance at winning the point. However, with such a confined court in doubles play, even pros screw up once in a while and strike balls that should have been let go. More so in doubles than singles, the paramount objective in pickleball is rushing up to the kitchen line and winning most points at close range. Fear of being inept, being hit, and being slow-of-foot are some of the "excuses" beginners make. But all players should be strongly encouraged to approach the kitchen line as quickly as possible, especially in doubles. The served ball is returned deep, and then the returner SHOULD start making the net charge. The server, after letting the ball bounce, then has a choice of hitting the ball hard down the middle or down the line, lobbing, or hitting the proverbial third "dinky" shot, especially if the returner is already perched and waiting at the NVZ. So, getting to the NVZ line is important, regardless of the level of play. But it can be tiring for the elderly to continually slog toward the net while crouching the whole time. Pickleball looks easy and poky from the sidelines, but repetitive motions can be back breaking and rapidly exhausting. Whereas tennis allows for goodly runs and then rest periods, in pickleball the smaller court area concentrates the twisting, turning and quick sprints - movements that can become quite fatiguing in a hurry. Backing off the kitchen line or never getting there is a notorious pickleball no-no. Former tennis players with excellent eye-hand coordination can get away with half-volleys, but not pickleball novices with no previous racquet skills. Once the NVZ line is toed, please stay there. Sometimes a beginner player will get pummeled, other times she will miss gimme volleys or makeable dinks. Nevertheless, it's crucial to take the initial "hazing" and to become fearless and proficient around The Kitchen. Hitting the ball too hard, whether from the baseline or at the NVZ line is a matter of debate. As stated before, no one appreciates a "woodpecker" opponent, even if popped-up balls should be rightfully swatted down. Developing finesse and proper ball placements are applauded hallmarks of advanced play. However, the sport is evolving, and I have seen a greater propensity for hard first strikes when returning serve, blasting balls directly at vulnerable opponents at net and a seeming disdain for dinking ad nauseam, even if the pros still do it. Who knows, pickleball and tennis strategies may be slowly and unfortunately merging, whether the elite pickleball purists like it or not. Lobbing is a very effective strategy, but only if the ball lands out of reach of the opposing players and lands inbounds. And those are big ifs. All players seem to get annoyed at the constant lobber who thinks that's the way to win. And although effective, especially against short players, lobs must be hit accurately and that does not always happen. In brief, I have touched upon some of the DON'Ts in pickleball that can elicit insulting remarks and cause already irritable players to become even more irate. And that applies to doubles partners as well. It can be so tempting and well-meaning to "educate" someone who has an exasperating game. However, the rules, racquets and balls keep changing. The sport of pickleball itself is changing. Who's to say what tomorrow's new game will look like or how players will execute winning points? A stalwart partner who you make disparaging digs at today may someday turn around and say, "Hey Boomer, shut the fuck up and learn how to half-volley, lob and… stay the hell back." You never know.

13

Who Covers the Middle?

Oh, boy. This is one of those awkward and sometimes maddening aspects of the game that really needs to be figured out between doubles partners prior to playing. The alternative is quickly articulating out loud if an oncoming ball is hit slowly or softly. However, due to twosomes often forming haphazardly during pick-up games, it is often difficult to get into positive synchronization. Or to trust your "new" partner to know whom is ultimately responsible for opponents' shots down the middle, which most adversaries aspire to hit. Usually the forehand has preference, but I have played with enough bottom-dwelling pickleballers to know when to wisely back off and have my "ball hog" partner swipe at the ball backhanded rather than risk having my head chopped off. I have had countless close calls, my racquet literally slammed out of my hand, and suffered bodily injury playing with stupidly aggressive doubles partners who "think" they have *game*. Just sayin'. Again, that's my observation and not an overt insult. I'm not disparaging novice players who are genuinely trying hard and still learning. It is also true that advanced players can get in each other's way, as well. Nevertheless, as one advances up the pickleball ladder of skill, one notices purposeful hits and kitchen play (NVZ), besides the obvious kill shots. There is a certain cadence and flow to games, a rhythm method (I like how that sounds) regardless of the ad hoc-formed partnerships. Of course, seasoned doubles duos that play together regularly as a tournament-ready team are even better synched with each other and often look smooth in their shot creations, lack of unforced errors, and have less clanging of paddles in the middle of the court! So, who covers the middle portion of the court during heated play? Well, it depends, but conventional commonsense and pickleball wisdom dictates that the forehand gets preference, whether hitting back the dinks, slams or center line shots. But what if one of the partners is a lefty and both forehands face the middle? That's a tough call. And, who runs back to get the perfect lobs placed down the center? Well, probably the chump who is most physically fit betwixt the two.

14

Paying the Price

This could also be appropriately titled: Dinking and Getting Doinked! What am I talking about? Let me explain: As mentioned elsewhere and ad nauseum in this alleged comic novel, when learning the sport of pickleball, the touch-filled ability of willfully hitting the ball (dinking) into the opponent's No-Volley Zone (kitchen) to eventually set up a kill shot is eschewed in doubles as the preferred and artful way of playing. Really? Maybe among the elite and pro players who have deft touch and bountiful skills. But you would be hard pressed to witness such dexterity and playmaking at the amateur lower levels. Ha, ha. What a joke. And although very proficient at dinking, I have unfortunately been doinked many times with the unforgiving pickleball by beginners and mid-level doubles players who didn't get the memo that less is more and that there is beauty and sublime elegance to the soft and flaccid game. Although perhaps I shouldn't have used those particular two words in that last sentence when describing the elderly male dink! On many occasions, when playing with a wide range of lower-ranked participants I have executed a brilliant dink that you would think could only be returned with another dink but instead been rudely blasted (tagged) by the ball from a player that just hit it back at me hard, with no regard to form, function or finesse. And then the blank stares begin, from my partner as well as the opponent who targeted me. All parties give me the slant-eye as if to reinforce their habits that dinks don't work, that I am merely a prima donna princess and pompous pol for even attempting one. Ha, how dare I try something that only advanced players and pros routinely use? "Just hit the fuckin' ball," seems to be the beginners and intermediates mantra when playing. Of course, whenever I level up and play with my advanced "dawgs," the subtle dinking game is paramount and of great importance when setting up and winning most points. It can be a physical chess match and a test of wills, skills and consistency. And all that concentration, bending over and back-breaking scuttling back and forth from just behind the kitchen line to gently massage the ball and keep it in play for many exchanges can be extremely fatiguing. But I persevere nonetheless, constantly slowing down the "novice game" and hopefully convincing the players around me to accept the validity of the dink and not always be tempted to smash away on every shot. However, whenever I play amidst a plethora of non-advanced players, I make sure to protect my face with my non-dominant hand when approaching the net, or at least to be ready for a blast that I know is coming sooner or later; mainly sooner.

15

Not Jekyll, Just Hyde

There is always that one a-hole, widely known to most local pickleballers, who not only acts out inappropriately when missing shots but is of churlish character in general. The kind of nutcase that people have to walk on eggshells around. His unprovoked "bad" behavior could almost be excused if he had been an advanced-level participant; however, no. Not only was his pickleball prowess questionable, but he sought to blame everything and everyone for his shot-making shortcomings. You never knew when an angry outburst was coming. Playing doubles alongside or against him while accepting the derogatory running commentary also could have been better tolerated had it been benign, self-effacing and truly humorous. However, that was not the case. He really meant what he said and some of the uttered words were unnecessarily hurtful. Ennis was known to me prior to my venture into pickleball. I had unfortunately tangled with him while playing competitive table tennis at a local ping pong club decades ago. While relatively skilled in table tennis, he was even then a troubled and nasty fellow who not only hated to lose but would petulantly leave the table at a moment's notice and then vacate the premises. What a pompous jerk. Now, I respect tough and challenging competitors in any sport and even those that throw tantrums and rackets out of frustration, but I will not put up with rude and crude insults directed at me or others, even from an "overheated" athlete. Ennis and I exchanged words many times and almost came to blows on a few occasions while he was losing to me via the ping pong ball. Luckily, he did not throw hands - it wouldn't have ended well for him. Most other players at the club let him get away with insolent remarks and actions, but not me. I hate malevolent bullies! Anyway, with the unwritten rule of congeniality being among some of the unusual hallmarks of pickleball, Ennis definitely did not fit in and was often an unwelcome pariah amidst local players. And then after years of "playing and complaining," he mysteriously disappeared, at least from the popular indoor scene. Good riddance. I guess his enormous ego eventually figured out that he was persona-non-grata. Duh! Nevertheless, if I ever encounter Ennis on a pickleball court again, I will purposely antagonize him with choice words and sharp shots. Why not? And I will pity that fool if he decides to start something physical with me….

16

Player, Entertainer or Both?

I admit that watching WWE Raw and Smackdown on TV for years has probably warped my mind somewhat – it's basically soap opera drama with ritualistic and acrobatic "wrestling" thrown in. Baby faces (good guys) and heels (bad guys) perform scripted, stuntman-type, choreographed moves where no one really gets hurt. Nevertheless, the extreme agility, acting and tumbling abilities of the actors (talent) can be breathtaking and highly entertaining. And the personalities involved…. Ha, that's where MY pickleball game comes in. It started in tennis with wild shirts and socks and has now morphed into a more eccentric and eclectic "WWE-type" of persona that I am slowly experimenting with. Nothing too outlandish but I am always pushing the envelope and will hopefully carry that concept to future tournaments, as well. And at my age, why not? Why not engage in a little audacious entertainment? I'm not a paid pickleball professional or *real* comedian so who cares? Well, perhaps the tournament directors and serious-minded, pro-wannabes, but so what? With a natural and lengthy gray beard, buzzed scalp, mirrored retro Steampunk sunglasses on my scowling face and a black towel hanging over my head like a prizefighter - not to mention the bodacious shirt, shorts and socks that I wear - my latest visage resembles an intimidating, toxic personage of unapproachability and potential danger. Not a full-fledged a-hole while playing, but as a slightly sinister, obnoxious, overbearing, and hopefully amusing individual before and after games. But even that is subject to change as my overall tournament demeanor and alter-ego continues to evolve. And if I get *canceled* in someone's mind, so be it! Of course, right before play begins – and like a toad shedding its skin - I quickly remove some of those outward trappings for a baseball cap, sports goggles or "normal" sunglasses, if playing in the sun. It's mostly intentional pre and post-game *performance art* with cheeky shenanigans on my part. Some knowledgeable folks say that my DDS

(Doctor of Dental Surgery) degree should have been supplemented with a concomitant DDE (Doctor of Dental Entertainment) certificate upon graduation from dental school, but that's a different story altogether. And let's not forget my intentional shirt changes between pickleball games; all the t-shirts have multiple colorful markings and outrageous messages on them to at least annoy some onlookers. Hopefully the apparel is barely legal and serves to offer amusement to most fans and players without overly offending purists of the sport. Because there are ALWAYS some of THOSE types present as per usual. Hopefully I will never press anyone's buttons too deeply and elicit a stern reprimand or ejection. However, and in addition to the above-mentioned visual effects and my usual self-demeaning banter, I always play hard to win. I play fairly and honestly although a smirk, a smile and retort will usually emerge should a comical situation arise. "Did that ball bother you? Take a first serve," is also a common shout-out to my sometimes befuddled serving opponent should a ball from a nearby court interrupt our game. All levity aside, however, I am also playing to take names and kick ass. Ha!

17

Singles Play

For whatever reasons I was never a big fan of doubles tennis, either as a spectator or participant. Sure, my high school doubles partner and I went undefeated during my senior year, and I tolerated it. I won a few USTA-sanctioned doubles titles as an adult at the local level with different pals of mine, and I tolerated that. And I have played my share of doubles pickleball – that's how I initially learned the game! That said, I am not some aloof lone wolf. I take personal responsibility seriously in my racquet sports and love singles competition overall. Be it table tennis or formerly plain old vanilla tennis, singles is the "bomb" for me. And, so, I took that feeling into pickleball and now enjoy one-on-one battles much more than doubles action. However, unlike tennis, singles and doubles pickleball are distinct from each other, with differing scoring, strategies and movements required. And now a few words about singles play: Playing east-west is the first and easiest singles strategy. Jerk your opponent to the right and left and keep her moving. Hit nothing down the middle, just back and forth into the corners if possible. In other words, "Hit the ball to where they ain't!" Secondly, combine that tactic with hard hits or heavily top-spinned balls. Next up is the "moving-forward" approach. Judiciously running up while your opponent is awkwardly reaching for a ball is ideal, even though some advanced players will return most shots. I personally prefer to bang from the backcourt rather than willfully approaching the net unless I can virtually guarantee myself an easy put-away shot. Another avenue of play is the drop shot/lob style. I have witnessed singles pickleball players hit dinks and then lobs in succession, and then over and over again. However, the pickleball court is much shorter and narrower than a tennis court, and physically fit fellows have no problem racing down those types of shots and then hitting their own balls for winners. Nevertheless, as the age ranges creep up, sometimes those abrupt shots can be effective, especially against players who no longer have good on-court mobility. Next up is the player who seeks to rush the net at every opportunity, resembling the serve-and-volley tennis player of yesteryear (a la McEnroe). Kind of like most of the current professional pickleball players out there. But, because of the Double Bounce rule, the pickleball server cannot immediately advance forward after serving to volley the ball out of the air. However, one CAN run up as soon as possible after carefully placing the third ball, and then hopefully knocking off the fifth shot. By contrast, savvy receivers can return the serve (second shot) and then charge the kitchen line and volley for a Side Out. Servers can be at a seeming disadvantage because of the chip-and-charge tactics of an

aggressive returner. But there is
something relatively new on the
horizon: Bashing the ball hard and
directly at the oncoming opponent in
hopes of an easy block-back shot which
then can be maneuvered for a winner.
In summary, the baseline-retriever
mode of playing may work in tennis
but not so much in pickleball. A few
points may be won this way, but
running back and forth is difficult, if
not overly tiring. Sometimes young and
energetic players utilize this form of
play, but for many older folks this is not
reasonable or warranted. Get to the
NVZ and put the ball away, before
your heart gives out! As I have
mentioned before, my opportunistic
and offensive style is to keep moving
forward as warranted. If it's a deeply

returned ball, I stay back and return it back deep and with placement as I bide my time. If it's a short ball I drive it or dink it, and then come on in. If mercilessly attacked and pinned at the baseline I try to pass, lob or hit the ball hard directly at the opponent. Nevertheless, sometimes proper placement of the pickleball is more important than slamming it. Anyway, I basically TRY to induce the opponent into hitting uncomfortable shots, ones that hopefully will come back to me short or in the middle of the court. Then the goal is to dictate the next series of hits and win the point. I also try to run around my backhand and hit forehands; it was a former tennis weapon of mine and I utilize it as needed. I slice it, hit it flat or topspin it, never giving opponents a chance to hone their strokes against one type of shot. Keep them guessing, I always say. My forehand drives are accomplished using the shake-hands Continental grip, unlike the Semi-Western grip I employed in tennis. And much like I did in tennis, I DO switch grips from forehand to backhand, with the backhand grip being Eastern. I tend to volley with a hybrid of an Eastern and Continental hand-holding grip, sort of between the two. Hopefully I have not confused anyone by now. I encourage beginners to ask a pickleball teacher/coach how to hold a paddle and effectively strike the ball in order to achieve maximum results. Lastly, most novice pickleballers wish to work on weaknesses, such as dinks and backhands, and that's fine and dandy. But don't forget about improving the intangibles like stamina, running speed, overheads, etc. And don't forget to cross-train in other sports, just to exercise unused muscle groups and to stay in shape. Of course, round is a shape! Lol. Conventional pickleball doubles wisdom dictates hitting down the middle and at the opponents' feet. But not so in singles. I find it better to keep the feet of competitors out of the equation and hit into open spaces or behind the player. And I ALWAYS try to size up the competition as quickly as possible, namely, do they have a good forehand, backhand, etc.? Do they appear to be quick around the court? Are they already sucking wind after a few practice shots? But that's me. Ha, perhaps I should shut my trap and let the "professional teaching books," video tutorials, and pro instructors do the talking. I mean, what the hell do I know? Some people say that I just happen to have an ounce of sporty talent left over in my dotage that I parlayed into successful pickleball. But beyond that "I got nothin'!" So true, although….

18

Still Trash Talking

Somewhere in this book I expounded on the guy whose bellicose on-court belligerence was uncalled for and unappreciated. But am I also close to being a tiresome loudmouthed jerk with a geared-up Gearbox paddle in hand? I surely hope not, and I try hard to keep my allegedly "funny" banter between points to a minimum, especially when playing doubles. Some players are more stoic than others and don't wish to listen to crap for the sake of me getting a few cheap laughs. However, many situations tickle my funny bone and then my addled brain has words pour out of my cake hole, usually to the amusement of the surrounding hoi polloi. But not all. It's those determined and serious folk that I have to remind myself to lay off of. Additionally, it seems that the highest rated amateur players are tight-lipped and appear stern as compared to the "average" ones. Maybe rightly so, perhaps their smug and arrogant inner egos have swelled along with their skillsets but remain internalized? Anyway, most pickleball players have a good time in their own ways, and I have learned when to keep my trap shut, no matter the levity in front of me that is virtually begging for color commentary. Trash talking at sanctioned tournaments is another animal, however, and I usually take it to a whole new level. Although competitors, including me, are usually friendly, my gloves come off during singles events. Wearing "loud," obnoxious shirts, and saying choice, pre-event ludicrous statements about phony injuries, my "novice" status and alleged tiredness before striking the first ball, are examples of the stand-up act that I deliver when competing. Some fellow opponents have chuckled at my faux sincerity, some have believed my deadpan deliveries, and some have allegedly complained about my verbal antics to the tournament directors. Oh well, a little psychological gamesmanship goes a long way and it's all in a day's work for me when slapping that pickleball around when it truly matters – going for the gold medal, baby! Although a fierce competitor in all my sports, past and present, a little humor here and there helps me to relax and enjoy the moment. Some of my favorite expressions that I like to utter on the court just prior to a tournament-level match are: "I'm just a beginner." "Take it easy on me. I just started playing last week." "All I have is a soft and flaccid game." "Do I have to hit the ball back to you?" And during warmups I purposely feign weakness and let my opponent hit the ball past me a few times before saying, "Wow, you're a great player, hope I can hang with you with my bum leg and all." "I'm just a fat old man." "Don't hit so hard, I'm already exhausted!" and my favorite: "I just don't have it today." Now, some competitors that already saw me play earlier will smile, laugh or sarcastically call me out and tell me that they know what's coming. Others get fooled, hopefully giving me a disarming mental advantage. However, all that being said, I am the first player - in singles or in doubles - who will genuinely praise my partner or opponent for hitting a winning shot. That will sometimes confuse the players involved because of a recent sardonic outburst from me. Nevertheless, I am always generous with line calls and give honest compliments when good shots are struck, regardless of who strikes them. But I also never apologize for winning a net cord dribbler that goes in my favor, frequently exclaiming "Yeah, Baby!" out loud while obnoxiously pumping my right fist and awkwardly kicking my right leg up into the air (a la Elaine

Benes dancing on Seinfeld). More head games from me, as always. However, if the net cord winner goes against me, I will merely say, "Bad form," and grimace in the general direction of my opponent. If one of my shots just misses and gets called out, I will often say, "That's a varsity call right there," or "That's a veteran move." And some more from me after winning a contested point: "I just got lucky. It hit off my handle," and "I don't have that shot. Sorry, it won't happen again," knowing full well that I do have that particular shot, and it most likely will happen again! Another favorite is to blurt out, "Let HIM feel my pain," if an opponent misses an easy ball. And when having lost a long point in the hot sun, I will sometimes loudly exclaim, "Figure it out, Minnesota Fats! He's running circles and trapezoids around you. It's a track meet out here!" But when a contested point goes in my favor while I am mounting a comeback I will enunciate, "It ain't over. Start singin', FAT BOY!" If a shot by my opponent is badly missed, I will sometimes say, "No way Jose," with the accent on the first syllable (so it sounds like Ho'-Zee). And if an opponent tumbles on the court, my usual response will be "Upsidasium" (A word used instead of uranium throughout the titular Cold War episode as part of "The Adventures of Rocky and Bullwinkle" TV show), or "Get a ref." "It's hammer time," is also a fav, especially if it is time to stop a losing streak and get back to winning. And then to add, "Okay, Rudolph, full power!" But after missing many shots in a row, out comes, "I forgot how to play!" And then there are line calls: Oftentimes a ball will miss by a hair on my side, and I will of course call it out. However, using my hands, I will often facetiously indicate to my worthy foe that it was out by a mile: All part and parcel of being perceived as a puckish pariah on the pickleball court. Although I accentuate the "funny" rhetoric during tournament play, I firmly believe that my snarky snide remarks have not only elicited laughter from adjacent onlookers and players but have greatly helped me win various and multiple state Senior and Masters' Singles Pickleball Championships at the highest level over the last few years.

However, I could be dead wrong and have instead angered, needlessly aggravated and wronged a lot of steadfast elderly men who are fed up with my bawdy outfits and inane loquaciousness. Perhaps most are itching to put me in my place in upcoming singles events. Or just plain itching. We'll see who gets the last laugh, and it might not be me.

19

Harmful Habit or Healthy Hobby?

This depends on which side of the "racket" fence you are on, and maybe you're on both? In essence, most exercises or sports are probably beneficial for the individuals indulging in them. But what about the "average" man-on-the-street, condo-dweller or non-athlete (NARP)? Must they suddenly have to put up with holey *noise pollution*, the wholesale occupation of large swaths of indoor and outdoor spaces by boatloads of old people clutching pickleball paddles, and possibly endure the ensuing mental FOMO? Is pickleball helping some while inadvertently harming others?

Let's discuss: For as many encouraging newspaper articles that have been recently published to promote the effervescent sport as a healthy hobby, especially for the elderly, there have been just as many deleterious ones that expose pickleball as a potential menace. For the uninitiated, uninformed, and complacent couch potatoes out there - and even tennis players - the invasion and seeming hubris of this loud and bold behemoth of a sport can be overwhelming. It's kind of like the invasive Gypsy moth (now renamed the Spongy moth) that causes foliage infestations and devastation, except with no end in sight! Heretofore unseen and unheard senior citizens seem to appear like an unwanted swarm of locusts and overtake parks, tennis

courts and gymnasiums to play a daft
and slowed-down conglomeration of
ping pong/tennis while smiling from
hearing aid to hearing aid. WTF? The
old adage: "Yes, but not in my
backyard," seems to apply to pickleball
as of late. First it was a novelty, then a
pastime, and now a loud-ass sport. And
at the beginning of its spreading
popularity, it was welcomed writ large
to make tennis courts useful again (let's
face it, tennis is dying in America), and
as a "simple" game for oldsters to
partake in. But when the obnoxious
"popping" starts at 6 AM on the relined
tennis courts in the middle courtyard of
an apartment complex and continues
unabated through the night on
frequently lighted courts, then
pickleball may indeed be a nuisance for

many non-players. Some say the unrelenting "percussive pops" border on torture, not to mention the ongoing good natured and contented repartee of the participants. The nerve of "them;" human beings should not have that much fun. Sure, there have been attempts made to manufacture "silent" paddles, but even those can excrete ungodly sounds at ungodly hours of the day and night. In addition, property values have supposedly plummeted near pickleball venues. Kids and their parents have purportedly been left sobbing and angry when the asphalt surfaces of playgrounds are routinely overwhelmed by aggressive armies of cunning curmudgeons. Cul-de-sac and dead-end streets in somnolent neighborhoods have also been overtaken by obstinate old people who come armed with spray cans (to paint the lines with), and portable nets. All under the guise of healthy living and youthful aging. Really? Where are the police? Where are the senior center employees to round up wayward seniors? Aren't there enough mental institutions available? Good lord, when oh when will this gray-haired onslaught and ubiquitous scourge end? Those FOPs (fuckin' old people) are everywhere, damn them. Ok, Boomer, you can sit down now and get your excitement vicariously via a social app on your cellphone like the rest of the obese youngsters out there. What? You want to get out of the recliner, run around and hit a wiffle ball? What the hell is wrong with you? Rhetorical questions aside, hopefully pickleball will level off in its zeal to take over all racquet sports in a goddamn hurry, and peace and quiet will be restored where needed and requested. But just an aside, I have heard positive reports of housing communities being planned and built with pickleball courts in the mix. Go figure. But until the day comes when paddles or pickleballs are made of foam (yeah, right!), the cacophony will most likely continue in many locales and be a persistent irritation (like mosquitos or chiggers) to those innocents living there. Sorry, not sorry!

20

Addictive Obsession

As my pickleball journey continues, I reflect on what made this game so ultimately "addictive." Was it merely the dopamine and endorphin rushes like seasoned runners or drug-addicts get? Was that it? But why? Did pickleball somehow push all the right psychological and physiological buttons to make it the "ideal" pastime as well as sport? Questions, questions…. I had been playing for a while now and seemed to reach a comfort zone on the court. I was and am still improving but the main reason I was playing so much is because I was having a blast. It was so much FUN to hit that ball without getting too tired or grievously injured. And having fun seems to be the obvious answer. Plus, I NEED to play often to stay sharp and in the groove for tournaments, my other addictive obsession. A psychologist once said that humans are attracted to joy. Well, that statement pretty much sums up pickleball for many players. The Holderness family - of internet-influencer fame - make goofy videos and podcasts about a wide variety of subjects. And, of course, they have made more than a few funny ones about pickleball. In one such amusing video, the husband-and-wife team describe the five stages of pickleball: Judgement, Curiosity, Reluctance, Commitment, and Obsession. It's as if they talked to me first before shooting the humorous footage. They got it exactly right and realistically portrayed catching the pickleball bug. Humor aside, let's briefly examine why pickleball is so easy to become habituated to: It's easy to learn, one can always readily improve, it's a relatively cheap game and joining a tennis or country club is not necessary, there are different levels, co-ed play is encouraged, play includes singles and doubles, it's a very "social" sport, it's not as cutthroat as other racquet sports, it's slower paced than tennis, it's kinder on the body than other racquet sports, it has soothing "rhythmic popping" sounds, there is hitting without all the running, and all body types can play. In summary, what's not to like about this sport? If you want to get competitive, there are tons of professional and amateur tournaments to choose from. If you only wish to play sporadically at the local YMCA and do more talking than swatting, you can do that too. Lastly, if it wasn't for the obligatory scoring and vacating of courts so others can play, many happy and diehard doubles teams would stay and play against each other for hours…. It's a sport with a very wide coalition of participants, styles, levels and inclusivity. Pickleball is just plain FUN and if it is truly addictive, then so be it!

TIMEOUT!

21

Pandemic Pickleball

It doesn't matter what side of the debate people are still on. Some firmly believe that the deadly Wuhan Flu was accidentally released as a result of a "careless," gain-of-function viral experiment gone rogue, one that leaked out of a virology laboratory in China. Some folks insist the virus came from a putrid pangolin or rancid raccoon dog at a Chinese wet market. However, it makes no difference from whence it came: the ensuing and much politicized virulent infections and unacceptable death rate shook America to its core and caused widespread shutdowns, including the "American way of life."

And NOT playing pickleball during the early stages of the mandatory lockdown period was downright disastrous, too. Well, not really. Pickleball's a game where social distancing is the norm during regular play. The sudden closure of most indoor venues caused the outdoor version of the sport to blossom even more than before. People could play, exercise and easily socialize from at least six feet away from each other. While other sports suffered, pickleball seemed to become more popular during the pandemic. Uninfected family units and close friends could surreptitiously creep onto unused, pickleball-lined tennis courts, play unmasked, and then craftily sneak away. It became a bonding and sporty experience, all in one. Nevertheless, most, if not all, of the indoor facilities were shuttered making outdoor pickleball the only viable option. And as stated, I believe that the closures really propelled the sport forward. With so much time on their hands, even the younger crowd that was sponging off the government with pandemic-funded bailouts could now join retirees on courts and learn the game. Counterintuitively, it was a heady time with seemingly more and not less pickleball being played. However, I did lose contact with many die-hard pickleballers as the Covid crisis deepened. The bad times affected everyone differently and initially it was not the right time to rekindle budding friendships. It was every man and woman for themselves while trying to stay alive. I remember faithfully watching the news and daily death toll numbers. Those hand-wringing days were an anxiety-ridden killjoy and not an inducement to go out and get sick because of a desire for human contact. But pickleball in the open air proved to be a safe and great distraction. It caused my wife and adult son to really accelerate our pickleball acumen. We three became much better players because there wasn't much else to do except to isolate from others and bash that colored, plastic ball between ourselves. I had started playing intensely and regularly at the start of 2019 but by March of 2020 basically was forced to quit cold turkey, at least from playing indoors. Then I got my family involved and together we not only forged through the various waves of Covid but gelled as a pickleball playing posse. Each member pushed the others to keep improving. Finding outdoor courts was not a problem. We scoured the largely deserted tennis courts in our area and found ones that had pickleball lines painted on them (most had already been devoid of any tennis players for years), parked our car… walked on… and played. Gradually we saw others enjoying themselves with paddles in hand. Slowly, the outdoor pickleball scene picked up steam and by late 2022 I was back to becoming reacquainted with former pals and getting back into doubles as well as singles matches. And playing indoors as well. Nevertheless, since the pandemic, my family and I continue to prioritize our closeness and

seek to actively play with each other
first, before venturing out for pickleball
dates with others. It works for us.

22

Seasons Don't Matter

With the pandemic basically in the rear-view mirror, it was time to ramp it up and start playing regularly again. It did not matter if it was singles or doubles. It was still pickleball, dammit! "Honey, we're supposed to get two feet of snow today. What time are we playing at the Y?" I would implore my wife. "It starts at ten and we better get there early so we can play more than a few games. Good thing you put studded tires on the minivan," she answered back. And another typical wintry day would ensue in our household. It was ALWAYS time to play pickleball, no matter the weather or season; even climate change made no difference. We would methodically pack our large and logoed pickleball bags – similar to tennis bags – with fruit snacks, power drinks and water, check our gear, and then don winter clothing before exiting our house for the car. Because we happened to be playing indoors, we had our sneakers with us in the special side compartments of our respective, bulbous bags. We would change into them upon arrival at the venue. Most of our fellow players did the same. No one wanted salt or grime on the polished gym floor from soiled boots. Now, you would think that snow, sleet, hail, and God-awful winter conditions would dissuade the masses of picklers from going out. Ha, ha. My wife and I would open the gym door and there were already four doubles teams playing on the two courts, paddles stacked up the wazoo in the corner, and crusty veteran players either sitting or pacing, but ready to play. And we got there early, darn it! Everyone gave us a fist bump, greeting or smile as we sought the limited seats available, put down our bags and put our kicks on. This was a near daily occurrence. Same routine, same place, same people. It was comforting in a way…. During the summers it was virtually the identical paradigm. Showing up at the various outdoor park tennis courts (which no longer serve tennis players) was the norm for us as it was for all the area's determined players. Although some preferred indoor play to avoid the sun and wind, I did not like to mix outdoors and indoors because as previously stated, they are almost different games. However, even I broke that rule on occasion and reluctantly went indoors to avoid rain or gale-force winds. Anyway, it was always nice to see and talk to people we had not seen in a while as well as to reconnect with the same cusses we just played against yesterday. Most of the play is of a co-ed variety, first come-first served, and doubles only. It can be quite challenging to get a singles game going, what with all the hungry peeps chafing at the bit to play. Oftentimes singles players (like my family and me) have to wait for long periods until the courts are truly free, or travel to find clandestine outdoor courts or lined indoor floors in obscure locations. All to be able to practice and play with likeminded people without guilt or time constraints. Do we play too much? I don't think so. "Honey, there is a tornado warning in our area today," I once matter-of-factly stated out loud. "That's okay. Let's hit the Y at ten sharp and get some hits in. You know those crybabies will probably close early because of a little breeze," my wife shot back. Upon arrival, through threatening skies and blustery conditions, we quickly walked past the concerned-looking YMCA staff and into an overflowing gym stuffed with our smiling comrades. Perhaps we do play too much? Nah!

23

Naysayers

While pickleball is enjoying worldwide admiration and participation, there are the tennis purists and pundits who wish to knock it down a step or two. Because many tennis courts have already been "desecrated" and marked-up by sacrilegious pickleball lines, meanwhile tennis clubs have been inundated by pickleballers, some in the tennis camp are protesting the seeming "takeover" of their beloved sport. I don't blame them - I used to be one of "them." The vitriol and animosity launched toward pickleball is typical: "It's a poor man's tennis." "It'll never catch on." "It's for fat fucks who can't play anything else."

"It's for AARP members who are slow as shit." "Underhand serving is for babies and grannies." "Tennis has devolved into hitting a goddamn wiffle ball." "It's for wannabes who couldn't cut it in professional tennis (actually that is true for Ben Johns and a few other current pickleball stars)." Even some old school and retired tennis superstars of yesteryear have piled on the anti-pickleball bandwagon and admonished the sport as a non-sport suitable only for unfit Sunday hackers. However, there have also been a few publicized and televised pickleball matches between celebrities and former tennis champs. And most of the participants, in doubles and singles, stated afterwards that they were surprised at the effort required to achieve a high level of play. It seems that even the so-called vocal naysayers have begrudgingly given pickleball a tacit bit of approval and respect. It's not like tennis has stayed true to its original roots. No professional tennis player is still playing with wooden racquets, using the Continental forehand grip, hitting with white balls, or wearing long sleeve shirts and pants on court. Sports are created and evolve, and I'm sure pickleball will not be the last athletic endeavor to cause rancor among other racquet-wielding enthusiasts. Onward and upward with pickleball. With rule changes and the constant tinkering of paddle surfaces, the original sport may be unrecognizable down the road - that's only natural and to be expected. And I also expect the PPA (Professional Pickleball Association) to become more populated with retired tennis pros who still want to hit a ball without further damaging their already worn-out bodies. To the naysayers who are sick and tired of having tennis courts commandeered by marauding hordes of mostly senior pickleball players and to the people who can't stomach the popping sounds: well, it's here to stay I'm afraid. If you can't beat them, join them, I guess. I did, and I haven't looked back since. Do I miss tennis? I miss playing at an advanced level. I miss the competition, tournaments and hitting the fuzzy balls. I don't miss the bodily aches and pains and regression of my tennis skills as I have aged. I also don't miss the faithless finks I used to regularly spar with. I guess I could have swallowed my pride and played at a lower singles level or switched to doubles only. But no. In pickleball, I can still vanquish opponents in singles that are half my age, so to speak. And I can still sprint short distances, swat that pickleball with full power and not feel beat up afterwards. Perhaps it is my bloated sporty ego talking or a normal evolutionary and age-related progression for me? Most likely both. But let's face it, I still like to win while having fun and pickleball has become my paddle-inspired vehicle to accomplish each.

24

Nude Pickleball

Even though I identify as a part-time naturist (only in the bedroom, shower, indoor hot tub, and while gardening), I am definitely not brave enough to take the next step and expose myself fully on the pickleball court. But nude pickleball is a "thing" and can be found at various secluded clubs and retreats as part of the worldwide naturist experience and lifestyle. There are many topless, bottomless and nude venues, including popular beaches found all over Europe. And I've heard that many clothing-optional adherents are truly liberated, Vegan, back-to-earth, down-to-earth and family-friendly folks whose bare backsides and parts and pieces seek to hurt no one. Nevertheless, when playing outdoors sans attire, would-be and seasoned pickleballers are encouraged to wear plenty of sunblock on exposed genitalia, and socks and sneakers are de rigueur. Now, I'm fairly certain that most true nudists are so accustomed to nudity that they actually enjoy the liberating feeling of not wearing clothing more than the implied sexuality offered by the naked bodies of strangers around them. However, what about the casual hedonistic man who identifies as a horny biological male, but thought he was *cool* enough to play pickleball in the buff at a toney resort while keeping his ego and manhood pointed downward? Well, "Here's the rest of the story," to steal the opening line from former radio personality Paul Harvey. The story goes that for a few days this fit and trim, middle-aged, hard-body had been doing alright, among misshapen, dumpy, wrinkled, and saggy-baggy seniors, until a svelte and perky hot babe graced the pickleball court one day. Holy hell, one glance and his temperature and other things started to rise and stand at attention. The gorgeous and strategically shaved female was opposite him as part of doubles play and try as he might, he could not keep his eyes off her. She, on the other hand, did not help matters by coyly smiling while staring at his "pickle and balls" that were flopping around in the air. Oh, it was highly embarrassing. I guess he did not expect her appearance to be so profoundly titillating. In the end, our "hero" literally ran off the court, complete with his bobbing member, to grab a towel as concealment after the match was over. However, no one had said a single shaming or derogatory word during the game or even afterwards. And the beautiful woman, who was his erectile nemesis, "disappeared" from the resort never to be gazed upon again. And our gentlemen friend? He played unclothed for the rest of his stay and managed to keep things in check and without anymore "on-court" issues. So, what is the takeaway for a heterosexual, cis-gendered, highly sexualized, uninitiated "male" newbie who desperately wishes to play nude pickleball? Masturbate profusely prior to playing in case feminine beauty arouses more than your suspicions? Drink lots of alcohol to hopefully dull the senses and induce softness? Find a resort with old and decrepit nudists only? Do the "deed" on court with a willing female hottie to "get it over with" and then resume play? Practice tantric and stoic sexual ideology and think about other things while staring at exposed, bouncing titties? Some of the above? Wow. I'm not sure if nude pickleball is for me! Now, that short, evocative and seemingly salacious tale was not metaphorical, allegorical or wishful thinking. It was a true story, but not mine. Although, I can easily commiserate wholeheartedly with that unnamed poor chap. Freedom from restrictive garments and the thought of 24/7 nudity may have their open-minded appeals; nevertheless, I think I'll keep my shirt and shorts on, for now.

25

Jargon

Who knew that there would instantly be certain words and phrases associated with the "new-fangled" sport called pickleball. Well, I didn't know, but eventually found out about most of them. In addition to my own sarcastic mutterings and self-deprecating rejoinders during play, I have yet to wholeheartedly embrace and enunciate some of the "official" lexicon of pickleball. And I have noticed that others have not been overly forthright to "name-drop" pickleball idioms either. Perhaps it's the particular region of the country I live in. Maybe my crowd is ignorant? Or introverted, and shouting out supposedly funny retorts is beneath them and embarrassing? I don't know. But suffice it to say that besides my allegedly "humorous" responses to amusing situations, most on-court banter involves score keeping, verbal compliments, and/or barely audible swearing. But I will at least mention some of the common as well as colorful slang used by some pickleballers. Thankfully, much of the ostentatious lingo is not uttered in this part of New York State. Dinking, the Kitchen, Side-Out, 0-0-Start, Ace, Body Shot, Spinner, No Man's Land, Pop-up, Half volley, Overhead, Poaching, Lob, Slice, Tweener, and Foot Fault are benign-sounding and fairly familiar refrains heard in my neck of the deep woods. And most were usurped from tennis.

But what about Andiamo, Pickled, Flapjack, OPA!, Dillball, Falafel, Chicken Wing, Corkspin, Stacking, Nasty Nelson, Erne, Pantry, Quinned, Scorpion, Shake and Bake, and Basher Bob? Now, speaking about the latter sentence, I'm sure there are additional descriptive and outrageous words that are a growing part of the sport. The ridiculous verbiage may make the game more interesting-sounding and give players a sense of exclusivity and arrogance when talking about it in front of newbies or the uninitiated. But is it getting out of hand? I don't know. Personally, I think "pickleball" sounds silly enough. But that's just me. However, my buddies and I certainly don't use any of those supposedly bona fide yet obnoxious terms. By the way, all of those "pickleball words" can easily be searched up, so I won't describe them here. Finally, perhaps the sheer fun of the sport lends itself to such ludicrous, tongue-in-cheek humor and name-inventing? Pickleball can be played seriously or not, and at many levels. And if a new slogan pops up that floats your boat, perhaps use it the next time you play. For instance, going to Bruegger's Bagels (a regional bagel shop) means winning a game with zero points scored by the opposition. You know, getting bageled. But you didn't hear it from me.

Touching Paddles, Etc.

Pickleball winners and losers frequently extend pleasantries at net at the conclusion of games and then engage in something tennis players do not – lightly touching paddles as a sign of goodwill and friendship before departing the court. During my tennis playing days, most losers were sore losers and would not even extend a hand for the customary after-match handshake before skulking away. In pickleball, there is this unspoken rule of camaraderie built into the sport that EVERYONE abides by. Although I admit that sometimes the habitual tapping of paddles between doubles partners after points can be annoying, the end-of-game paddle-bumping is a soothing pomade no matter the final score between previously contentious combatants. It has become a rite and ritual of the game. And after all, besides the pro players and a few tournament-minded amateur butt nuts like me – who also touch paddles - pickleball is still widely regarded as a fun activity for the aged, with the emphasis on FUN. Winning and losing seems to lose its meaning for most elderly folks, even if they had one-time championship-level prowess in other sports. In conclusion, the civility and etiquette extended to and by opposing players demonstrates the uniqueness of pickleball and I hope that tradition continues. And another thing that makes pickleball genteel and friendly-like: The unwritten rule of allowing walk-on players into the playing rotation during open play, regardless of ability. Now, this most often applies only to doubles and usually the walk-on player has enough sense to park herself by players of her level, if there is a choice. And unless there is strict league or sex-delineated pickleball involved, I have yet to see a would-be pickler turned away during open play. That kind of inclusivity and kindness is a far cry from what I experienced back in the '70s during the heyday of tennis. On many occasions my old man and I would seek to play at packed public high school courts during the cool, summer evenings. Newly posted, huge placards indicated that playing time was limited to one hour and that respective players were on the honor system. Yeah, right. As if by magic, and with smirks on faces, every single queried twosome or foursome insisted that they had just arrived and would be leaving in exactly an hour. Sometimes we would go home without hitting a ball because it got too dark to see even the white balls we used back then. However, Dad and I were the same. We would never, ever leave early or invite interlopers into our midst for doubles or singles action during "our" time, even if we knew them! However, to be fair, perhaps it has something to do with the length of typical games involved. A tennis match consisting of at least two sets usually takes much longer to complete than two typical pickleball games of eleven

points each. But that's how tennis is.
Thankfully, that's not pickleball.

27

Injuries?

I know, I know. How can old geezers that are barely moving get injured? Right? I mean, low-level doubles pickleball is as forgiving as it gets. What with light plastic balls that hardly bounce or fly, a cramped court where running is the exception and not the rule, and a slow pace of play…. Sheesh, I'm getting sleepy just writing about this…. Now, now, I am only joking, or am I? In reality, skeleto-muscular and nerve injuries can and do occur in most sports, regardless of the alleged passivity involved. Golf and baseball, though not contact or sprinting games, always seem to have injured players in their ranks.

The same goes for pickleball, mainly in singles and due to the overall fragility of the many oldsters that play. But injuries can happen to anyone of any age and at any time. In pickleball, unexpected falls, scrapes, being whacked by a partner's paddle, taking a smashed ball to the lip, and twisting of ankles and artificial joints are but a few examples of what can befall the unprepared or ignorant. During my halcyon tennis days, taking time off to heal after "getting hurt" was the norm. Heel spurs, multiple fractured metatarsal bones in feet, rolled ankles, sprained wrists and elbows, shoulder bursitis, sciatic leg pain, bruised toes, etc. were common and to be expected. Nevertheless, in pickleball, the higher the level played and the higher the level exerted during play will lend itself to more physical trauma. It's common sense, I think. The more advanced I have become and the more singles I have played have led to more episodes of plantar fasciitis, pulled hamstrings and calf muscles, shoulder and elbow issues, and overall bodily exhaustion. Maybe forgetting my age and thinking that this bitter old prick can play like a twenty-year-old has something to do with the periodic and sporadic injuries that plague me. But overall, it is rare to witness a sudden or debilitating illness or serious impairment caused by pickleball. I am sure there are some, and I stand corrected if I have overlooked the fine folks who have been sidelined by inadvertently stepping on a ball or getting a ball to the eye hole. My sincere apologies (watch where you step and wear eye protection).

28

Tournament Time!

Yup, that photo represents not only my tournament mindset, but an intimidating slogan I often display when it's "hammer time" and time to lay it on the line. I stop SOME of the foolishness before the opening serve and then try my darndest to win, baby!

Gone are SOME of the usual on-court mannerisms and audible trash talking; singles tournament play is crunch time and I can get seriously serious in a hurry. Of course, I am never truly silent while playing…. And now for a few saliant words about actually participating in tournaments and the headaches involved, as well as a slightly philosophical discussion on the sublimated and egotistical thoughts of still being perceived as a "winning athlete" even at a ripe old age: To the casual pickleball enthusiast, enrolling in sanctioned competitions, singles or doubles, might be the logical next step in the evolution of playing and a source of fun and accomplishment. The ensuing anxiety of performing while under pressure can be exhilarating, especially if winning medals is a goal (strangely, trophies are not awarded at most amateur events). However, it has been my observation that players who do best in a stress-filled, cutthroat tournament environment are the same ones who were once highly competitive athletes in other sports. You know who I mean. The toughies, former jocks (male and female) who always rose to the occasion and loved to win. That's not to say that "ordinary" folk might not enjoy the atmosphere of a tournament, but it takes a special kind of *chutzpah* and mental attitude to sign up in the first place. Mostly it's the same rotating bevy of well-seasoned and hardnosed pickleballers who go from tournament to tournament, much like WWE performers going from town to

town as part of their wrestling "circus."
And I am no exception. After a
"lifetime" of playing in amateur tennis
tournaments, it was only a matter of
time (my wife was right) until the "call
of the wild" called again and suckered
me into the competitive genre of singles
pickleball. But first, and true to my
lifelong love of WWE wrestling, I have
decided to embody an intimidating
bad-boy, "heel" persona as part of my
entrance-*schtick* at tournament venues.
The picture in the back of the book will
be my current "competition look." I
will not actually play with that get-up,
but it'll be a *trip* to walk around and be
stared at as a pseudo-psycho pickleball
player who seems angry and not to be
trifled with. And if I get into someone's
head – good. It's all part of the game; at

least it is for me. And my new *playful* pickleball nickname is "D R ZACH," a play on words on my real name and former day job. But let's talk a little about the actual jousts. However, first a few quick words about the victuals and liquids that are necessary when competing. I prefer bland and non-controversial foodstuffs, such as plain hotdogs on rolls without condiments, plenty of available Gatorade-type energy bars and gels, and lots of water and Gatorade-type drinks. Everyone brings coolers stuffed with sustenance and it takes practice to pack the stuff that will actually be consumed. Okay, back to the story: Like in tennis, it has been my unfortunate experience that most pickleball tournaments are not smoothly run affairs. The various and harried administrators wear many hats and have to constantly sift through ANTICIPATED and UNANTICPATED problems when running a large event over a usual three-day period. Some players fail to show up, some old duffers have died since signing up, some levels only have one participant, some doubles teams are suddenly missing a partner, and so on. Woe to the newbie participant who expects perfect court conditions, perfect weather (indoor or outdoor), perfectly timed rest or bathroom breaks between matches, and a perfect performance while playing nerve-wracking games. One time I played a major state senior event where there were two squeezed-in pickleball courts per tennis court with inaccurate pickleball lines taped on with peeling BLUE masking tape on a BLUE background. *Oy vey*! Another time, sunglasses and sweatbands had to be worn in outrageously humid indoor conditions because of the hot sunshine pouring in at an awkward angle through the large windows and reflecting off the newly polyurethane-lacquered hardwood flooring. Wearing a cap tilted at an angle against the solar array did not help. And yet another time I thought of wearing cleats because the indoor, YELLOW-painted floor was so slippery, and YELLOW Onix balls were used. Good Lord! Even advanced players could hardly run without slopping around and could barely see the damn ball. One time there were so many lines from other sports painted on the court surfaces that it was hard to distinguish where the pickleball lines were. That resulted in tons of testy arguments because of the bad line calls made that day. Duh. And then there is the added bullshit of unfamiliar surroundings, unfamiliar foes, crappy cash-catered food (it's better to eat your own tender vittles while playing), strange balls that you have never used before, and the dictatorial ministrations of the frazzled director trying hard to cleverly combine age groups and levels on the fly so that everyone at least gets a chance to play one match. The combining of age groups and levels into one giant category, such as age 60 and over for level 4.0 and above, seems to be the norm and is a common "bait and switch" routine plied on the dupes that signed up. I mean, it can get downright frustrating and aggravating. I have not been to a tournament yet, major or minor, where everything was *Kosher*, or ran as smoothly and accurately as the slick, online sign-up page claimed it would. So, why do I do it? Although usually traveling together with my adult son - who as mentioned before doubles as my attorney, coach, trainer, physio, and biggest *athletic supporter* - why do I drive long distances, stay overnight in expensive motels and put myself through hell to play singles pickleball against strangers who strangely interest me? Why do I wantonly waste fossil fuel – much like those annoying activists/hypocrites Al Gore and John Kerry – just to travel to distant destinations? And all without any monetary compensation? I mean, I did the same thing in tennis years ago. I guess it's who I am and HAVE to do it. The need for speed is real, to paraphrase a visceral racing analogy and metaphorically apply it to pickleball. At first it was a way to test myself against the very best at a high level and in my age group. After I passed the tests with flying colors, my familiar lust for winning had me shoehorn tournament pickleball into my overall "combative" being. Tournament play is not for everyone. However, for me, it's part of life. So it costs me a bit, so what. I love to compete. What can I say?

29

Disclaimer

I wish to formally apologize to tennis players everywhere. The noble racquet sport seemed to bear unnecessary ridicule and verbal ire from me during my seemingly flippant conversion to pickleball. And a half-hearted apology to most of my previously stalwart cache of feckless tennis buddies who showed their true colors when they abandoned me en masse. Additionally, I'm sorry if I tended to be longwinded and on a high horse when describing the "dos and don'ts" of pickleball as well as some of the colorful characters playing it. After all, I'm not a professional pickleball player or a psychoanalyst, respectively.

Nevertheless, playing pickleball has been a mostly pleasant experience for me and hopefully I have not ruined the game for would-be and existing players with my "delusions of grandeur," confessions of gamesmanship, bushwhacking style of on-court horseplay and dubious levity.

30

Last Words

I was a lifelong tennis player who anticipated practicing and competing 'til I could barely walk. However, unlike my old man who played competitive tennis into his late eighties, that day came sooner than planned. Well, not really: I can still ambulate at a brisk pace and to date have no artificial joints. Nevertheless, in December of 2018 – at age fifty-eight and after my third knee arthroscopy – I suddenly realized that I could no longer play SINGLES tennis at my customary high level. Overnight I seemed to have become brittle, old and tired, and my long-term tennis buddies abruptly resembled a toxic bunch of bozos. With a few exceptions, I was so done with that insincere mob of miscreants (in hindsight my astute wife had accurately referred to my *lame* group of tennis chumps as the Psycho League). And in an unexpected turnaround, my wholehearted and half-century love for the game simply vanished. Plain and simple, playing tennis was NOT fun anymore. Fortuitously, pickleball was there to pick me up: spiritually, psychologically and physically. It wasn't love at first sight, but slowly developed into an immersive, family-friendly sport and escalated with my participation in advanced-level SINGLES tournaments, albeit age-appropriate ones. And unlike my extended experience with the local tennis scene, the pickleball community is filled with inspirational and wonderful folks. Most have no axe to grind or to stick into your back! However, who knows what tomorrow will bring? In a cruel "twist of fate" or "twisted bliss" (thank you Jeff Hardy and Alexa Bliss, respectively of WWE fame), years, months, and days seem to pass quicker after reaching a retired elderly state. With that in mind, there is no time to waste because clocks keep on ticking and seniors unfortunately keep physically wearing out. Therefore, get out there and at least swat some pickleballs before it is too late! And one more thing: throughout this book I have equated pickleball with the word FUN. And it's so true. That said, I would like to announce here and now that I will play pickleball until the bitter end, however, that kind of naïve arrogance may be a bitter pill to swallow at the end. Perhaps I will still be alive into very old age and playing at a high singles level, or maybe I will become a decrepit dullard and succumb to dreaded doubles play, or even resort to cornhole and outdoor shuffleboard to get my jollies. In any event, who knows when I will finally have to put down my self-customized pickleball paddle and stop hitting those *unholy*, holey balls....

Thanks for the read.

About the Author

Dr. I Mayputz (not his real name) graduated with highest honors from high school, pharmacy college and summa cum laude from dental school. After completing a master's degree in prosthodontics at a then prestigious institution, he embarked on his career in private practice. He is now retired. As an elite Master's athlete, he has won various championships in singles tennis, sprinting, snowshoe sprinting, javelin and singles pickleball. In addition to being a verbal artist, naturalist and part-time naturist, he is also known as a caustic wit and provocateur. Dr. I. Mayputz has previously published comedy novels using his pseudonym as well as released numerous nature articles in regional journals under his real name. Additionally, he has authored multiple scholarly pharmaceutical and dental abstracts and written many children's books, also under his given name. Lastly, he wrote this book to entertain family, old friends, fellow pickleball players and any curious sod willing to vicariously *experience* the game of pickleball.

For more alleged levity by Dr. I. Mayputz, please read:
Dental School: A Bizarre Comedy
Pharmacy College: Crazy Daze and Hazy Nites
Elementary School: Wits and Twits
Junior High: The Muddle Years
High School: Buffoonery Central
Dental Delirium: A "Humorous" Look at Dentistry
Retired... And I'm Still Tired!
Drugstore Delirium: A "Humorous" Look at Retail Pharmacy

"D R ZACH"

"Saddle up bucko. It's gonna be a bumpy ride!"